Notes towards Recovery

Copyright © 2019 by Louise Ells
All rights reserved. No part of this book may be used or reproduced in any manner whatsoever without the prior written permission of the publisher, except in the case of brief quotation embodied in reviews.

Publisher's note: This book is a work of fiction. Names, characters, places and incidents are either the product of the author's imagination or are used fictitiously, and any resemblance to actual persons living or dead is entirely coincidental.

The production of this book was made possible through the generous assistance
of the Ontario Arts Council.

ONTARIO ARTS COUNCIL
CONSEIL DES ARTS DE L'ONTARIO
an Ontario government agency
un organisme du gouvernement de l'Ontario

Library and Archives Canada Cataloguing in Publication

Title: Notes towards recovery / by Louise Ells.
Other titles: Short stories. Selections
Names: Ells, Louise, 1967- author.
Identifiers: Canadiana (print) 20190054085 | Canadiana (ebook) 20190054131 | ISBN 9781988989082 (softcover) | ISBN 9781988989099 (HTML)
Classification: LCC PS8609. L5725 A6 2019 | DDC C813/. 6—dc23
Printed and bound in Canada on 100% recycled paper.

Book design: Nine 29 Design Studio Inc.
Cover Artwork: Peter Finney
Cover Design: Heather Campbell and Laura Stradiotto
Author photo: Catherine Holden

Published by:
Latitude 46 Publishing
info@latitude46publishing. com
Latitude46publishing. com

Notes towards Recovery

LATITUDE 46
PUBLISHING

Written with love for
Margie (1962–1971)
Dad (1923–1999)
Aunt Joyce (1913–2012)
Aunt Em (1940–2017)

"Memory is the way we keep telling ourselves our stories - and telling other people a somewhat different version of our stories."
Alice Munro

Table of Contents

SUMMER

Erratics 3
Melting 19
Scraping 35
Grafting 43
Mirrored 51
Moon Jellies 61
Family Tree 73

FALL

Surfacing 83
Riffle 97
Granny Squares 107
Fiddleback Symphony 123
Fruits of the Nightshade Family 131

WINTER

Milk Rime 137
Push 149
Northern Lights 157
Turbulence 169
Preservation 179
Notes towards Recovery 191

SPRING

Stained 199
Dispatches 209
Whale Song 229

Erratics

I wonder what's left, if there are any proper cottages around the lake. I see pictures of Muskoka now, its multi-storey mansions with all mod cons: air conditioning, televisions, Wi-Fi, wrap-around decks, three-car garages. When is a cottage no longer a cottage? I think, and feel old.

I'd like to imagine ours might have survived. The outskirts of Muskoka. On an island in one of the unfashionable lakes, too far north of Toronto. I won't go back to that part of Ontario; I'm not willing to risk not recognizing the area, not willing to risk missing the correct turn-off. I don't want to discover the gritty gravel road to the boat landing has been paved and a Tim Horton's has replaced the chip truck in the nearest town. I choose to keep the cottage exactly as it is in my memory, exactly as we left it.

A 'flood of memories,' people say. I can imagine that, if I drove north: my being carried away on the crest of a tsunami, then pulled under, unable to see through the water's thick, through the onslaught of surfacing memories.

Our cottage was called Lee's Word - a play on my grandfather's name, Leslie Ward, with a nod to the crossword puzzles he wrote,

Notes towards Recovery

published every morning across the country, which funded the land purchase and building of the original wood cabin. He seemed to value the pun enough to ignore the fact that his land was on the windward side of the island. Never mind. It was where my father had spent all his childhood summers and I spent the first fourteen of mine.

Swimming, canoeing, campfires, the occasional bear, loon calls at dusk. Reading novels on the dock, and Mad magazines, and playing marathon games of Monopoly by coal oil lamp, taking care not to burn the wick. There is a second-hand bookstore in Goderich I pass when I take my mother out from her care home, pushing her chair along the uneven sidewalks. As soon as the snow melts, they put out tables of books, and I'll sometimes stop, pick one up and open it, holding it close to inhale the smell of those summers. Sunshine and mustiness and shared history. I tried this once in the city I now call home, but it didn't work - the seaweedy salt air held other peoples' memories, not mine.

I was five years old the summer Peter was a baby. His crib was set up in the other tiny upstairs room, at end of the hall, as far as possible from my own room. Every night he stood up in his crib and cried, and I positioned myself in the doorway of my bedroom, watching and standing guard in case he was kidnapped.

To my young girl's mind it seemed possible that someone might paddle across the lake in that darkness, dock the canoe and creep along the path through the woods, scale, somehow, the shingles of the cottage to the second floor and open the window to cross the creaky landing and lift my baby brother from his cot, then repeat the whole journey in reverse - without alerting my parents who were sitting in the screen porch downstairs, sometimes reading, more often playing cards with the Jameses. The scent of their cigarette smoke curled up the side of the cottage, along with bursts of laughter, Dick James' political rants, his wife's shush-shushing.

Then, I knew nothing about teething, and because I was so quiet and my parents followed their generation's trend of allowing a child to cry itself to sleep in place of mollycoddling, they would never have come upstairs to see what was wrong and would never have known the role I played - albeit inadvertently - in keeping him awake and prolonging his noise. I knew enough not to go downstairs, not to make a sound myself - bedtime meant bedtime and the only acceptable naughtiness was reading under the covers with a flashlight.

Peter was the most precious thing in my life and I could understand easily why someone would want to steal him and keep him as his own son (in my mind it was clearly a man doing the kidnapping). I was too young to read the newspapers but perhaps I'd overheard the tourists at Lakeside Lodge talk about the missing American baby.

Later, I'd read about the Lindbergh case in one of the Reader's Digests that lined the bookshelves of every privy on the Lake. But by then I would have known that brothers could disappear in moments. Brent, five cottages along, had been in the Laser that tipped yards from the shore. When his sister, Heather, and the other two teenagers righted the boat and got back in there was no sign of him. They dove, they searched, they called for help, but his body was never found, not even by the Marine Unit that came all the way up from Toronto with scuba gear. Heather's parents returned, year after year, spending longer and longer at their cottage. They hoped her brother might have hit his head on an underwater rock, Heather confided once when my parents had paddled over to the Lodge for supper and she was babysitting Peter and me. Suffered amnesia, but survived and, one day, would remember his family and the summer cottage and return. Her

5

Notes towards Recovery

mother heard him, Heather told me. She said when the wind blew in from the north east, which almost never happened, her mother swore she could hear him calling out her name, waiting to be found. That spooked me and when Mum came home that evening I asked her to choose a different babysitter next time.

The next summer Peter was a year older and he fell asleep instantly, after days spent trying to keep up with me on his chubby little legs, and I realized my job was no longer necessary or urgent in the way it had been. And the summer after that I was allowed to stay up later, for s'mores with the gang of kids my age, or games of Scrabble with Mum and Dad before Dick and Betty James arrived for what had grown into a nightly ritual: drinks, snacks, cards, and a heated discussion in which the world was put to rights, interrupted occasionally by tourists who couldn't read the lake at night, didn't know how to navigate by cottage lights and had lost their way back to the Lodge. There was once a canoe, I remember, and two women giggling. I snuck out of bed and looked down; one of them was still wearing her swimsuit - a bright pink bikini and gauzy cover-up; she looked like a Barbie doll. She was twirling her blonde hair round a finger. "Easier if we take you back," Dick suggested, "eh, Bob?" My father must have agreed, as I soon heard the James' motorboat - a new purchase, first on the lake - start up, and when it had faded, the sound of Betty sniffling, my mother comforting her. The motorboat didn't come back for hours, and the next day there was a silence between my parents.

Those summers. Back in the city Pete was a boy and I was his significantly older sister and we had less and less in common. But at the cottage we were best friends. Us and all the full-timers; we were friendly enough to the kids at the Lodge, but they were there for a week or two, three at the most; there was no point spending hours together, sharing too many secrets, exchanging addresses and promises to write (though every summer I met at least one girl with whom I did just that).

It was a Lodge kid, though, an American, who discovered the jumping rock. He'd got lost, taken a wrong turn on the portage that linked our lake to the next one over, and come out at one of those dead-end lakes, too small to bother canoeing, bullrushes on one side and a rocky outcrop on the other. But he'd launched his canoe, looking, he later admitted, for a short cut back to our lake. When he'd paddled across he saw a giant grey boulder, a glacial erratic it was later decided, because of how different it was from the rest of the rocks in the area. With smooth sides, and a flat top accessible by a series of ledges, it was perfect for diving. That afternoon, when he took us back to the site, he claimed he'd done it, actually dived from the top, but I don't think any of us believed him. You'd have to be with a crowd, egging you on. I wouldn't even go to the edge of the top platform to look over, I was that scared.

Somehow it was agreed that it was too dangerous for anyone under twelve. "Aww, that means you can do it but I can't," Peter said. "No fair."

I was smart enough to take a way out when it was offered to me. "Don't worry," I reassured him. "I'll wait till you're twelve too and we'll do it together." But every day we went back with the other kids, watched the older ones leap over the edge, screaming, and disappear into the dark blue water. When they surfaced they laughed at their daring, at the risk, and clambered up to do it again. If our parents wondered where we were, why we were taking picnic lunches with us every morning, they didn't ask. It was summer, this is what we were supposed to do - be outside playing, getting fresh air and exercise.

Notes towards Recovery

    The Lodge kid was in tears on his last day of vacation and made us promise we'd name this awesome place after him. I'm sure we agreed; certainly we went to the landing, en masse, to see him off - barely recognizing him in long pants and a button-down shirt, climbing into a fin-tailed Cadillac for the nine-hour drive back to New York. He wouldn't have been out of Haliburton before we were back at the newfound lake, and before the summer's end, we'd broken our vow to him and re-christened the boulder The Jumping Rock. What we did keep was the rule that no one under twelve was allowed to jump.

    Two summers after that - I was almost fifteen, Peter just ten - Dad was promoted to principal and lost his three-month-long summer holidays. He'd drive up to the lake Friday night and head back to the city Sunday afternoon. We saw less and less of the Jameses and when we did, Dick, still a Phys-Ed teacher, always made a crack about Dad having joined the dark side. Even I noticed how strained the laughter was, but I didn't care; I had more freedom and that meant the chance to flirt with Stephen, a boy who'd mostly ignored me before. Sometime in mid-July, Mum replaced Betty with a new cottager. She came by most afternoons, sat on the dock, and the two drank white wine spritzers and held tinfoil under their chins to help their tans along.

    Peter was desperate to jump from the rock. I've no idea why we all clung to the belief that twelve was some magic age, but I pulled rank as his older sister and refused to let him do it. Still, that's where we went on days we weren't learning to waterski, or canoeing to the far end of our lake and back, or over to the landing from where we walked the three miles to the crossroads which comprised a gas bar, chip truck and ice cream stall. I was aware, that summer, of my breasts and legs, and had a bikini and a pair of cut-off jeans shorts I wore whenever I thought we might be hanging out with Stephen, who teased me in public but kissed me when we were both sure no one else was around. I sat on the edge of the platform at The Jumping Rock and Stephen sat next to me between jumps, sometimes squeezing me against to his cold, wet body. I'd squeal and pretend to pull away, while leaning closer.

There were a couple of weekends when Dad didn't come up. The first time he phoned the Lodge; there had been a bad accident on Highway 11, traffic was backed up for more than twenty miles, he'd been stopped for two hours and then given up and turned back. I was the one who got the message but as I was finally allowed to go to the teen dances at the Lodge, I didn't deliver it to Mum until after all the slow songs were over. When I paddled home to tell her that Dad wasn't coming, she sighed. Not angry or sad, as I'd expected, but disappointed, resigned. It was the first time I thought of my parents as a couple in the way I was starting to think of Stephen and I as a couple.

One of those perfect summer evenings. It must have been a Saturday; Dad was there, he'd arrived with rib eyes for the barbecue, and it must have been late August - no mosquitoes and already a hint of fall in the air. We ate down on the dock, plates perched on our laps, steak with potatoes baked in the coals of the barbecue and Mum's famous Cobb salad with blue cheese dressing. My favourite meal, the one I requested every November for my birthday though it never tasted as good back home. Dad had bought a fancy bottle of red wine too - "Get used to extravagant gifts," he whispered to Mum, "there may as well be some perks to this new job." I remember wondering if this had been the cause of the rift between Dick James and Dad - the sudden difference in their salaries?

Notes towards Recovery

We had blueberry pie for dessert, also on the dock, then Peter suggested we play Charades, a game we hadn't played in years. We acted out book titles, movies, sayings; at some point Stephen paddled by to see what I was up to and he joined in. Then he taught us a hilarious Mexican game where the trick was to come second. Winners were the losers, based on some Mayan tradition of sacrificing winners to the gods by throwing them into a cenote; I don't remember the details but our laughter must have carried across the lake. I suppose it only feels as if that was our last happy evening as a family because it was such a good one.

We'd planned to go up Thanksgiving weekend, like we did every year, but Pete had started hockey training and had a tournament. Mum stayed behind with him and Dad and I went up just for Friday and Saturday, so we'd be back in time to watch two of the games and for the turkey dinner on Monday. I had hoped Stephen would be up; turned out he wasn't one for writing letters and I'd not seen him since Labour Day weekend. He wasn't there. No one was, apart from the Jameses. The Lodge was still open - its final weekend of the season - but there were only old people, no kids. When Dad and I had finished all the end-of-season chores on Saturday morning I took a book down to the dock, but it was too cold to sit and read. I thought about taking the canoe out for one final paddle of the season but couldn't be bothered, so I walked around the island path and picked a few mushrooms. When I got back I needed to use the outhouse so I guess Dad didn't know I was there, didn't know I could hear them when he and Betty James met up. The conversation, the kissing, the plans for what - I understood, clearly - was a regular lunchtime rendezvous at the Inn on the Park.

The whole drive back home I kept my face to the window, my eyes closed. I practiced confronting him, telling Mum, finding the James' Toronto address and telling Betty, no- telling Dick, no-telling her and Dick. In the end, I didn't tell anyone anything. At the cottage I could have spoken to Peter. Not in the city.

Late March and spring had come early so we went up to the cottage for Easter. Stephen was there with a new girlfriend. I watched them paddle by, refusing to wave or in any way acknowledge their presence. Betty and Dick James were up, too, and invited us for roast lamb on Sunday. Mum was cooking a chicken for Saturday's lunch and wanted us out of the too-small kitchen so shooed us off into the canoe.

"D'you think Dad's acting a bit weird?" My brother asked me as we went towards the landing.

"He and Betty James are having an affair." It was the first time I'd said the word out loud. "I'm pretty sure Mum and Dick both know about it, too." I wanted him to ask me what was going to happen, if our parents were going to get a divorce, but instead he made a big J-stroke, swinging the canoe towards the portage.

"Let's go to The Jumping Rock," he said. We carried the canoe through the late winter woods - still snow, but a few patches of left-over autumn leaves and maybe the suggestion of trailing arbutus - crossed the water, pulled the canoe up onto the shore, and climbed up to the platform on top of the grey boulder. I guess I knew, had known as soon as he'd turned us away from the landing, what Peter was going to do. He stripped off to his swimsuit and sat down again.

"It's gonna be freezing cold," I warned him. Then, "are you sure it's safe?"

"It's safe," he said. "How many times have we watched all the others jump?"

I had to concede, but told him he better not expect me to follow him in. Then we spent a while trying to remember the

Notes towards Recovery

name of the kid who originally found it. Something pretty geeky, we agreed. Stanley? Franklin? Amos? My brother stood. I'd watched dozens of kids make the leap, dozens of times, but this time I held my breath. He went over, yelling out, his arms flailing. It wasn't graceful; he was lopsided and decided to cannonball at the last moment but didn't quite tuck in fast enough. His feet and butt must have landed in the water at about the same time, and then he disappeared. I leaned closer to the edge, still holding my breath until he surfaced. He was gasping. "Fuck, it's cold, fuck, it's cold, fuck, it's cold." I'd never heard him swear before, and that shocked me as much as watching him try to move towards the shore with jerky, un-coordinated movements, barely able to hold his head above the surface.

I grabbed his clothes and quickly made my way back down to the water, ready to dive in and haul him out. But he'd managed to reach the edge and all I had to do was pull him from the water. When I passed him his shirt he reached for it, then dropped it, his fingers too cold to work. Crouched, huddled in a ball, his teeth chattering. I touched his back - the temperature of his skin startled me and I took off my fleecy, rubbed him down just as I had when he was a baby, I undressed him, ripping off his swimsuit and manoeuvring him into his clothes. Then I rubbed his back again, and his arms, until his teeth stopped clacking against each other.

"Hey," I said then. "How was it?"

He turned to me and grinned with blue lips. "Awesome. Frickin' awesome."

"And you're the youngest ever to have jumped." Now that he was safe I was ridiculously proud of him. "Gonna do it again?" I was joking and we both knew it.

"Yeah," he said. "In July when the water's not so frickin' cold." We laughed and he lay out on the rock, palms down, pulling warmth from the stone. "Hey." His inflection made it clear it was a question.

"Yeah?"

"Just want you to know, I'm not gonna hang out with Stephen this summer. And that girl is a lousy paddler."

It must have been the sweetest thing he could think to say, and I loved him for it.

"You are the most awesome eleven year old I know," I said. "And my best brother ever."

"I'm the only eleven year old you know. And the only brother you've got." He flicked my arm, grinned again.

We sat for a while, then made our way back to our lake and back to our island and our cottage, neither of us in any great hurry. My contentment was broken by two things. Stephen and his girlfriend canoeing along the shore. She called out in a really friendly voice, but neither Peter nor I replied. And Betty James standing on the dock chatting to Dad when we pulled up. Did I imagine they both seemed flustered by our arrival?

"Oh my," said Betty. "Your hair is wet, Peter."

"He wins for first swim of the year," I announced.

"Oh my," she said again. "Well, I must be off. See you tomorrow for the feast. Bob. Kids."

"*Bob. Kids*," Peter mimicked as we walked into the cottage.

After lunch when we pulled the wishbone, Peter snapped off the longest piece and won. Again. He's a boy, he's stronger than you, said our mother. Subtext: he'll always be stronger than you, get used to it.

But that evening, when he was blowing eggs to decorate, and Mum was trying to act as if she wasn't already hiding chocolate for the next morning, and Dad was pouring himself another drink and wondering out loud if we should leave right after breakfast on Monday to avoid the worst of the traffic, and I was trying

Notes towards Recovery

to remember what homework I absolutely had to have done for school on Tuesday, and if it had been unfair of me to tell Peter about Dad and Betty James, his heart stopped.

He dropped the egg he'd been working on and it fell to the floor, cracked, yolk splattering on to a strip of my ankles, bare between tennis socks and jeans. "Oh for-" I started to complain, but then Peter hit the ground, smacking the floor, not moving, making no sound.

Mum screamed, but even as she was screaming, she lifted him and carried him, running, down the path to the dock. We followed behind, grabbing paddles, getting into the canoe, pushing off. And as Mum held Peter, Dad and I paddled towards the landing, the car, the phone box, the road. I remember moving the entire lake with each stroke, pushing it behind me, away from me, with such strength that the four of us skimmed across the water's surface. I recited the Lord's Prayer under my breath; it was the only one I knew.

Stephen's parents pulled alongside us in their motorboat and Dad told me to throw them our line and they towed us, too quickly for the canoe; it split in half as we reached the landing and Dad was soaked to his chest. Then the Jameses caught up, yelled at us to just start driving, they'd call the hospital. I suppose they took care of our busted canoe. And maybe it was Betty who righted Pete's chair, cleaned the broken egg from the floor, tidied away the chocolate rabbits and eggs in their obscenely bright foil.

There was no ambulance in those days and the nearest hospital was thirteen miles away. It was too late when we arrived. (It had, of course, been too late when we left.) A dickey heart, the doctor said. I remember that, dickey. A dickey heart. Undetected his whole life. A winter of hockey had probably weakened it, but it was impossible to know for sure.

My parents weren't like Brent's. They couldn't pretend there was any hope Peter was going to come home. My brother was going to be dead for the rest of our lives, from that Saturday until we were all gone and there was no one left to remember him. My mother tried to spend Victoria Day weekend at the cottage, but she couldn't. We arrived on Friday evening with a brand new canoe. All night I heard her crying, and in the morning she packed up a few of Peter's things to take home with her, and we left.

She said she'd try again when it was warmer, but as July first weekend approached she shook her head no, told Dad and I to go up ourselves, she needed more time, and needed this weekend to herself. Funny how little I remember. We would have gone to the buffet dinner at the Lodge, watched their fireworks display. Stephen was single again but I barely spoke to him when he stopped at our cottage and offered condolences, told me that he missed Pete too. After ten minutes of what must have been uncomfortable silence for him, he left. I believe Betty James came by as well and also left soon afterwards.

We should go home, I said to Dad, and he nodded. First thing in the morning he said. Then he sighed. Your mother and I have been thinking. Maybe we should sell this place. Sell it, I echoed, already adjusted to the idea. But not if you don't want us to, he said quickly. It's yours too, part of your history, and maybe you'll want to bring your children here. No need to decide anything just yet. I excused myself to go to the privy where I sobbed into a musty roll of toilet paper.

The next morning felt like my last chance. I crept out of the cottage in my swimsuit and took the canoe when the mist was rising from the lake and fish were jumping for flies. I walked the spider-webbed portage, paddled the short distance to the jumping rock, and clambered up onto the platform, planning to

Notes towards Recovery

run and jump before I could change my mind. But I hesitated, reached the edge and stopped. I imagined I could hear Peter teasing me, calling me chicken. I sat, then, and thought of the force of the glacier that had moved this boulder, of humans being sacrificed in underground cenotes, of the second last one being the winner. As if there could ever be a winner.

I don't remember any more discussion about keeping the cottage for my future children. I can't remember if it was sold before, or during, the divorce. It wasn't Betty James, but another woman Dad moved in with, and it was seven years before I returned to Muskoka. An August long weekend visiting a university friend's cottage; I was too close not to detour on the way home, and rent a battered canoe from the Lodge. I didn't paddle to the island to look at Lee's Word, but searched instead for the entrance to the portage. When I reached what I'd always pictured as a small lake, I discovered it had been claimed by beavers and was barely more than a pond. The Jumping Rock seemed taller, and much more dangerous - how had none of the kids hit one of the many rocks jutting from the water's surface? But I gauged the safest place to enter and this time I didn't stop, didn't hesitate.

So deep, so quickly. It was a shock - the bitter water, the dense waterweed - and I panicked, opening my eyes. In the dark I saw the suggestion of faces. As soon as I felt mud between my toes I pushed up, up back through the gritty, cold, water, gasping and choking.

I dragged myself to the edge, up onto the rock where we had sat that March morning. For several minutes, I focused only on breathing. Then I lay, palms down, just as Peter had done. The rock was cold, I continued shivering, and I cried out loud.

I took a job in Nova Scotia, where no one knew I'd once had a younger brother. Here, nor'easters are common. The sea never freezes, of course, but some winter evenings when I stand motionless I hear what Brent's mother must have heard: a moaning, from a great distance, far beneath the whitecaps.

Melting

That was the summer it didn't rain. By mid-June the corn was stunted and the hay was withering; on a breezy day my mother's laundry was coated with gritty red dust when she brought it in from the line. Old timers argued about the last time the river had been so low, and I watched streams fold in on themselves then disappear.

That was also the summer that Frank Tooley got it into his head to run a bus tour round our township. The previous year he'd convinced his Dad to try some new British beer, so he could enter a contest Brewers Retail was holding. He'd hoped for a dirt bike but instead won the Grand Prize of an all-expenses-paid trip to England. When he came back to school in the fall he wrote a speech for the Legion's public speaking contest about tourists, himself included, who were foolish enough to pay good money to sit on a coach and be told stories about things they couldn't see. "An empty field where perhaps a Roman Fort once stood. A wood where Henry the Eighth might have had a hunting lodge. A mound of earth that could have been a prehistoric Neolithic long barrow." His deadpan delivery had us all - judges too - in fits of laughter and I believe he went as far as the provincial finals.

Notes towards Recovery

He was a Bushie, Frank Tooley, all Valley slang and his brothers' hand-me-down hunter orange clothes, and he lived three miles out the wrong side of town. Neither a farmer nor a townie, he was destined for community college rather than university by dint of his father's alcoholism. Streamed through 'Technical' which meant auto mechanics, woodworking and plumbing, he and I hadn't been in a class together since grade school. But ours was a small city, only forty-three students in our year; we all knew each other.

He bought an old factory bus, one of the narrow double-decker ones that used to take workers to the mill back in the 'fifties when Robillard Pulp and Paper owned the town. He fixed it up, painted it bright green, wrote 'Landscapes of Our Past' on the side and ran his excursion with the same combination of cheekiness and good looks that had won him a position on the Student Council (with his promises to replace the hall water fountains with lemonade and change the mascot from a goose to a tiger so we could start winning some ball games). He nailed it; I guess pretty much every tourist passing through on their way up north, heading towards Algonquin Park, their cottages, and the scattered museums and attractions I was paid to promote, must have bought a ticket and taken a seat on his bus.

I took it first at the start of the summer break when I still clung to the promise a new beginning holds. I'd applied too late to join my best friend, Sally, on the bypass construction crew where she worked as a flag girl earning three times the minimum wage. Instead I was manning the so-called Tourist Information Bureau, a desk shoved into a corner of the town hall's lobby. I figured it would be one of my duties to be able to speak knowledgeably about the bus tour when asked, but Sally and I sat at the back and whispered through much of Frank's commentary. Sally worked out how much money she was going to have saved by Labour

Day and I worried that Aunt Lori had picked my younger sister to travel through Europe with her because I was too boring. You didn't have to come from the edge of town or wear hand me downs - there were other reasons not to fit in.

Sally tried to reassure me, but I knew. Not from Deborah's hastily scrawled postcards - so much left unsaid that I could only imagine sidewalk cafés, skimpy bikinis, midnight dinners at jazz bars - but because I had watched my baby sister grow up and away from me. Only thirteen months apart, when we were children we'd delighted in strangers mistaking us for twins. Now the differences between us could easily convince people we weren't related. While I was nervous and shy and worked at the art of being unnoticed, Deborah flaunted her quirks and was became exotic, popular. She had, of course, been the correct choice for a European odyssey with my Bohemian Aunt. I would have fussed about ordering museum tickets in advance, looking up train schedules, buying a phrase book for each county on the itinerary. Deborah and Aunt Lori claimed they had no plan, said they were making it up as they went along.

There was a booklet I sold for a dime which mapped all the town's points of interest: This is where the famous fire of 1918 started. Here's where the first settler squatted on land that he later bought from its rightful owner. There's the jail, with its original 1867 cell. There's where the last public hanging was held. But Frank Tooley was a storyteller, with no qualms about embellishing what meagre facts he had. After he'd done a circuit round the town giving details about the sites not found in any of the literature I had on display, he drove over the bridge into Quebec and down a dirt road, pointing out the entrance to the caves "where Jesuit priests over-wintered, kept alive by their moonshine," and the "magic rapids" that appeared for one week every seventh spring, and turtleshead portage. This, he insisted,

Notes towards Recovery

was named not after the flowers that grew there but two Hudson's Bay traders who fell asleep by their campfire and swore their bags of furs were stolen by giant turtles.

For the duration of the ride Sally teased me, claiming that Frank was putting on a special show for me. I shook my head, denying the possibility he was flirting, in awe of his self-confidence. For the passengers on his bus tour he played up his local roots, "that's one jeezly big Cathedral," he said, "but inside it's finer 'n frog hair."

Sally and I got off the bus and walked along the street arm in arm to her back yard, where her mother served us lemonade. We slathered our faces with baby oil to help tan our winter-white skin as suggested by one of Sally's teen magazines, and gossiped.

"Aileen McIntyre got a car," said Sally.

Aileen McIntyre. The coolest girl in High School. Remarkably, she and Deborah had become friends the previous year. I'd seen them giggling in corners of the school usually reserved for couples, walking shoulder-to-shoulder between classes, and Aileen had even been to our house for dinner a few times last fall. But something must have happened; after March Break I rarely even saw them at each others' lockers.

"Apparently it was a gift from her Dad for getting straight-A's."

When I took my straight-A report card home my parents had been pleased, but it was no less than they'd expected. My father, the high school principal, quipped that I took after him, but his joke fell a little flat because the unspoken corollary I heard was that if I was the brains, Deborah was the beauty. That my sister was gorgeous was a fact not even Sally could pretend away.

"I'm thinking of Med School," I said to Sally, and listed the universities I was going to apply to in the fall, hoping her list and mine might overlap.

"I'm thinking of an MRS degree." She laughed. "Seriously, Kathleen. School's out. I don't even want to think about it. I heard rumours about the bands that are coming for Summerfest."

Best friend though she was, there was some things I never told Sally, like that winter afternoon when I had arrived home from school, seen Dad's car in the driveway hours before he was due home, and no one had heard me come through the basement entryway. My mother and Deborah were shouting at each other with words so angry I couldn't translate them and in a moment of silence I heard a sound I'd never heard before: my father was crying. I stood motionless, then carefully re-opened the door and let it slam shut. "Hello," I'd called out, banging my boots as if to rid them of snow.

Mum had rushed downstairs, her cheeks pink. "Don't take your coat off, Kath," she'd said. "I have some errands to run uptown, come with me."

It was the only time she'd ever called me anything other than Kathleen. She hated nicknames and Kathy and Debbie were not allowed in our house, any more than alcohol, meat or caffeine. "If we had wanted to name our daughters Kathy and Debbie then we would have done so," she'd informed my first grade teacher in a tone that, at the time, made me squirm with embarrassment. Later it would fill me with pride.

We got into the car and drove along the length of Main Street. Finally I asked where we were headed. My mother shrugged, then swung the car to the right and out to the highway. "Why don't we have supper, just the two of us?"

"On a school night?"

"Two years from now you'll be off at university. Just once I'd love to have dinner with my sensible grown up daughter, just her and I. How about the Swiss restaurant? I've never been there."

Notes towards Recovery

For good reason, I thought. The cuisine comprised pork, veal and cheese. I assumed we'd leave as soon as she had looked through the menu, heavy as a book with a faux leather cover and each page coated with thick plastic. Instead she asked the waitress for a jug of ice water while we made up our minds.

She leaned across the table. "I'm sure they don't use rennet cheeses, you could try the fondue."

It was an incredible offer - cubes of crusty white bread to dip into thick, melted cheese seasoned with the lure of the forbidden. But she was playing with her wedding ring, pulling it up to her knuckle, then pushing it back to the base of her finger. I wasn't good with stress and I knew it would ruin the meal, that after a few bites I'd stop eating and the flame of the burner would go out, leaving a tasteless, grease-covered lump in the pot. So I said no thank you and ordered spaghetti with tomato sauce, and tried to make small talk for the duration of the meal, while Mum drank cup after cup of water and ate a few spoonfuls of soup.

"Dessert?" she asked. "Or look, they have root beer floats, your favourite."

I shook my head, no, watched her refill our water glasses. Our parents held strong beliefs, but they weren't crazy strict. I couldn't imagine what Deborah could possibly have done to merit my father's early return home from work, and far, far worse, his tears. In the past my sister had bought a leather coat, cheated on a French exam, been caught smoking a cigarette. None of those transgressions had resulted in my being disappeared for the evening. It had to be something colossal, maybe even criminal. Drugs? Theft?

It was late when we finally left the restaurant; the house was quiet when we got home and the only light on was the pale bulb above the stove, illuminating nothing.

Deborah never said anything about the incident to me, and I never asked, but the following week my parents told me that Aunt Lori had invited Deborah to go to Europe with her. "Leaving just the three of us together for the whole summer," my Dad said, as if that was my special treat.

That May, as soon as the last of the snow was gone and the top few inches of the soil had thawed, my mother decided to take down our childhood swing set to expand the vegetable garden. By mid-June the sprinkler ban had been introduced and all the lawns across town were yellow, but we carried water from the lake at the end of our road for the rows of bush beans, kohlrabi, zucchini, tomatoes and cucumbers. The simple chore became a ritual, first thing in the morning and every evening after supper - Mum and I pulling buckets of water on the red wagon from the lake to her garden, the lake to her garden. In the fall when we were putting up jars of pickles she corrected me, saying it wasn't her garden, it was ours. She hadn't grown the cucumbers, we had.

Our town was surrounded by farmland - the odour of alfalfa, corn and hay, and the stench of manure were always there; after I moved to Toronto I was surprised by the smell every time I went back to visit. It was only a fluke that we had a cathedral and thus official city status; a cathedral gifted by a man whose only child, a daughter, had sacrificed her inheritance when she eloped with an Indigenous man. Ironically, the plain brick building was most famous for a series of Indigenous paintings in which - according to the mimeograph leaflet produced by The Friends Of The Cathedral, copies of which I kept on the lopsided rack beside my Tourist Information desk - the creation myth of Gitche Manitou was depicted alongside the life of Christ. Having grown up in one of the few families that didn't sit in those pews every Sunday,

Notes towards Recovery

I delighted in visiting, tipping my head back to look up at the pictures.

Frank Tooley made the town an exciting place, if only for fifty-five minutes. I took the tour several more times, never telling Sally, because I didn't want her to tease me about having a crush on Frank, which I didn't. I loved being a tourist, a stranger, in the place where I'd been born and lived my whole life, hearing stories about buildings I'd never really noticed and spying over walls. The first time I saw the statue in the Chaput's back yard, a naked man and woman entwined in an embrace, I lowered my eyes, felt my cheeks growing warm.

I could see over Judge McIntyre's brick wall too and down into the garden with its private swimming pool, the only one in town. Aileen was there once, with her brother Rory, the Golden Son, home from his American University where he was playing scholarship hockey. I thought Aileen made eye contact with me, she grinned and waved, and then Rory shouted hello at the whole busload of passengers. "That's the home of Rory McIntyre," Frank ad-libbed. "This area has a history of hockey players who've reached the minor and major leagues-" he listed them all.

I studied the people on the bus that I would never see again. I'd never know what they would become. A young couple with three children and clearly a fourth on the way. A petulant teenager, seemingly determined not to enjoy a moment of the holiday with her parents. And an elderly man, apparently quite deaf - where was he headed that he'd stopped in our town and taken this tour? I felt sorry for him, the flakes of dandruff on his wrinkled collar made him look frail; I smiled at him and helped him down off the bus. For a moment I considered offering him a coffee, some conversation, at the soda bar in the pharmacy. But perhaps he didn't feel as lonely as he looked; maybe he didn't care about his old-fashioned suit and outdated hat.

It only took a couple of weeks for Sally, working outside, to perfect her tan and become part of an in-crowd I had no contact with. The strain between us grew into a rift when she asked me to go with her to the Summerfest dance and I said no. I tried, but couldn't, explain to her that it was easier for me not to go than to suffer the inevitable embarrassment of wearing the wrong thing and dancing the wrong way and saying too much or too little.

"Please, come," she said. "I don't want to be alone."

"You won't be." We both knew that was true; all the bypass workers would be there as well as the kids we knew from school. "Tell me all the juicy gossip when I see you the next day."

But I didn't see her the day after the dance, or for several more after that. When we did meet I was standing on the sidewalk on my lunch break, talking to Frank Tooley. She winked at him, then needled him, asking why he didn't include the Hermit's Shack on his tour, that was one interesting thing in this old town, she said.

"Derrick Lavalle. His name is Derrick Lavalle," said Frank.

Everyone knew the man paid kids a nickel a punnet for frog's legs and that's what he ate, along with squirrels, rabbits, and maybe a deer or moose if he was lucky. I didn't advertise the fact my mother took him fresh vegetables through the summer and hot meals every Saturday. She fretted about the still he kept behind his hut, but my father excused the man's drinking. It's to our shame, our shame, he said. Our country used him, damaged him and then abandoned him.

Frank felt the same way. "He's a war veteran, not a tourist site," he said to Sally, before leaving. I can't imagine he would have talked about poverty tourism, but the first time I read that term I heard his voice. We stood in awkward silence, Sally and I,

27

Notes towards Recovery

until I exclaimed at the time and went back to work to reorganize the piles of leaflets on the rack and scrub the desk top.

A week later I saw her walking hand-in-hand with a guy I didn't recognize, one of the road construction workers. I said hello, tried to be light and cheerful. "What's new?"

She turned away, as if she hadn't heard me, but I'd seen an expression on her face. "Tell me. Tell me."

She let go of her boyfriend's hand without introducing me and walked a few steps away. "Kathleen," she said. "There are rumours."

I smiled, then waited. She couldn't even look at me.

"Rumours?" I asked.

"About Deborah and Rory McIntyre."

"My sister and Rory McIntyre?" I laughed. "That's absurd. I think I'd know if my sister was dating Rory McIntyre."

Sally's cheeks were red. "Not- not dating, exactly," she whispered, unable to meet my eyes.

I didn't understand what she was implying. "Anyhow, she's in Europe for the summer, you know that."

"Is she?" Sally asked. "I mean, I'm sure she is. I'm sure it's all lies what people are saying, that your parents sent off her to one of those homes for unwed mothers."

Finally I understood.

"I'm sorry Kathleen. I didn't know if I should say anything to you. A bunch of people were talking at the dance."

A university student. A hockey player. Four years older and so far out of my sister's league. I knew my sister was wild, but I couldn't believe that she'd been intimate with anyone, especially not Rory McIntyre.

I didn't know how to react and nor did Sally. I couldn't blame her, but it was another wedge between us. Time with her boyfriend replaced time spent with me and as the July drought turned into an August drought with still no sign of rain, the blueberries, pinched and dry, withered on the bushes. Over before they began.

Frank Tooley's father owned three acres of overgrown evergreens. It had been one of his many schemes, this one a cut-your-own Christmas tree farm. But when it came time to harvest the firs, he said he couldn't do it. So he left them for a few more years, the pines and spruce and balsam, and then a few more, until it was clear they were far beyond Christmas tree size. Twenty some years on the trees were a scraggly mess, fighting each other for sunlight and blocking out any brush that tried to grow beneath. Without Sally to hang around with, I took to biking along the gravel road past the cemetery with a towel and a book, and lying on the needle floor of that cool haven, pretending to read. I breathed in the smell of shade and groused to the red squirrels as they leapt from branch to branch far above me.

"Unfair," I said to the squirrels. "Unfair that Sally's dating, unfair that when I go back to school in September for Grade Thirteen I will be exactly the same person who left Grade Twelve in May." The squirrels paused, as if listening, but then scampered away and resumed their chattering. "Deborah has been gone too long," I whispered. "I miss her." I held my hand on my flat stomach, trying to imagine a baby growing in my sister. Wondering what it felt like, making a baby.

Sometimes Dad and I went down to the lake after supper and swam away the day's heat that clung to us. I told him my dreams of med school and then we went back to sit on the porch to play Scrabble with Mum. The night before Deborah was due back Mum mixed frozen bananas, coconut milk and sugar with black specks of vanilla bean. Dad got down the ice cream churn from

Notes towards Recovery

his childhood farm, and we took turns cranking the handle and packing more ice and salt in the outer bucket.

"I bought some root beer," Mum said. "Why don't you invite Sally over?"

I didn't think I could do it, just phone her as if nothing had happened and invite her for a root beer float. "I don't even know if we're friends anymore," I admitted.

I couldn't say Rory McIntyre's name out loud, much as I longed for confirmation. On one my talks with the squirrels I had decided that as long as I said nothing to my parents then it was all just rumours that I could ignore. I changed the subject away from Sally, Deborah, Rory. "I was thinking, Dad, could we organize a work party this fall to give Mr. Lavalle a new roof? Is there a way to do that without him thinking it's charity?" The three of us talked about the possibility while we ate bowls of the ice cream, thick and rich and cold.

The next morning I still hadn't decided how to greet my sister at the airport or what I'd say, if anything, when we had a moment alone.

"Increase your word power: perturbation." Dad smiled at me across the breakfast table in an attempt to cajole me into a better mood.

But I was so restless that morning I reacted with silence, not even a sassy comment muttered under my breath, and in the end he drove down to Ottawa alone. I picked up a book, then put it down. Sat at the kitchen table and unfolded each section of the newspaper, pressing out the creases. Mum was making lemon meringue pie, Deborah's favourite, and the innocent smell of the lemon zest made my eyes tear. We both started when the front door bell rang, and Mum, her hands covered with pastry flour, asked me to answer it.

It was Rory's sister, Aileen. "Hiya, Kathleen," she said, as if we'd spoken only recently. "Can I come in?"

I said hello, thought of the breakfast dishes I hadn't cleared from the table, and the mess I'd made with the newspaper. "Mum's baking and the house is unbearably hot, let's sit outside in the shade." I led her to the deck chairs under the maple tree in our back garden.

"Busy summer?" she asked. "I saw you on that double-decker one day. I swear you looked just like Debs, even though I knew there was no way she could be on that old bus of Frank Tooley's." She laughed but all I heard was that, with the sun in her eyes, for just a moment, someone thought I was as pretty as Deborah. That and her casual use of 'Debs' to refer to my sister.

Flustered by her easy manner, the way in which she seemed to assume we might have news to share with each other, I stuttered. "Uh, well, I've been working at the Tourist Office. How was your summer?" I couldn't imagine what I could possibly have that she wanted and hoped she wasn't going to ask me if I knew anything about my sister and her brother's supposed intimacies.

She shrugged. "I hung out in Toronto for a while. Boring otherwise. You know this town." She smiled again.

I heard the kitchen door open and shut. "Is it too early in the day for a root beer float, girls?" Mum sang out as she turned the corner. She was carrying two tall glasses, decorated with paper umbrellas and blue striped straws; she stopped when she saw who was sitting on the other deck chair. "Oh, I- Hello."

Aileen said hello, but I noticed she was studying her perfectly shaped, pale pink nails as she spoke.

My mother passed her a root beer float, and me the other, and left. I could tell she'd guessed it was Sally at the front door, and I was suddenly sick that I hadn't mended things with my friend.

Notes towards Recovery

She should be the recipient of this unexpected treat, not Aileen McIntyre.

I took a long drink, the soda fizzing on my tongue, creamy and refreshing at the same time. Aileen only looked at the glass my mother had passed her, then set it down on the grass by her chair.

"I thought you guys didn't eat ice cream," she said.

"It has to be gelatine-free," I replied. Surely she hadn't come here to talk about my diet. I closed my eyes and concentrated on the cool sweetness. When I opened my eyes she was looking at me. "I heard you got a car," I said, to fill the awkward silence.

"Yeah. I can't wait to show Debs." She looked at her watch. "I was kinda hoping she'd be back already. Will you ask her to call me, as soon as she gets in?" I thought I saw in her eyes a plea.

I nodded and said sure and she stood then, knocking over her glass. The root beer disappeared into the lawn, the ice cream, already starting to melt, looked like a fried egg. I stood as well, and walked her to the end of the driveway, where she embraced me in a hug that took me by surprise. "Thank you," she said. "Thank you so much for not judging us. It is real, you know."

That was the last summer we lived with the dull background noise of machinery as it blasted through the rocky outcrops to the east and west. No one could have predicted the bypass would be finished three years ahead of schedule. And I don't believe anyone, truly, had realized just what it was going to mean for our little city. No more tourists drove along our main street, big box stores took over the farmland, and a Tim Horton's on the highway put three restaurants out of business, including the Swiss place.

Frank Tooley parked his double decker bus down the dead end road behind the area, where it sat for years, slowly rusting into an eyesore, used by teens as a drinking and smoking hang out, until the town council declared it a danger and had it carted off to the dump.

I chased those dreams of mine to the Big Smoke and discovered I was a better at being a doctor than a wife. Deborah and I grew closer when I finally realized what Aileen had been trying to tell me, what my sister had been brave enough to share with our parents, what a trip abroad for the summer had not disappeared.

We are back in town, Deborah and I, for our mother's funeral, and now that the house is sold I don't imagine I'll have much reason to return. After leaving the lawyer's office on Main Street, we pass the pharmacy, long since shut. There is no traffic but I look both ways, out of habit, and just for a moment glimpse Frank Tooley, his high school self, standing at the corner.

I blink; the street is empty.

"What're you thinking?" my sister asks me, turning to see why I've stopped in the middle of the road.

"That summer," I say. For a moment I forget she hadn't been here. She never boarded the green bus. Landscapes of Our Past. She can't imagine how surprised I was, always, at the end of the tour when I walked down the stairs and off the bus onto the sidewalk, this sidewalk. Always back in exactly the same place as I'd started.

Scraping

Staring back at the Nova Scotian shoreline we've left, I take shallow breaths through my mouth in an attempt to avoid the smell of engine exhaust and seaweed and the tub of dead fish for the puffins. Not a boat person, never a boat person - that was a love Daniel shared with Dad. I see him now, Dad, shaking his head and telling me to take deep breaths, focus on the horizon and look towards the destination, North Brother island, not the wind farm we're moving away from.

North Brother island is only a couple of miles off the starboard bow, but it's too flat to see, and this isn't a direct journey. A man from Parks Canada will meet this boat of puffin watchers when it reaches its port of call, over an hour away, and we'll retrace this passage back to the Brothers. It was the best I could manage to organize. It will be worth it, I promise myself, lousy as I feel, seeing the roseate terns. So high on Dad's wish list.

"Well, well," he'd said when he first read about it. It must have been in the quarterly newsletter he got detailing species sightings across the country. I remember the crinkly paper, pale blue, and my excitement every time I saw it our mail box. I read magazines online now, and scroll through social media, and feeling middle-aged, mourn the passage of that era when physical mail brought

Notes towards Recovery

pleasure. "Well, well. I grew up not thirty miles from the country's largest colony of roseate terns and had no idea. I'd very much like to go and see them, hear them." That would have been fifteen years ago, I was in my fourth year, home for Thanksgiving. Mum decided it was coffee time and the three of us spent the next two hours looking at maps and books, planning how to get to North Brother, stops along the way, then researching the birds. The Humming-birds of the sea Audubon had called them.

We all knew it was a fantasy, we all knew Mum wasn't going to travel again, but Dad and I refused to acknowledge the reality out loud. "June," he said. "We'll go in June for the hatchlings." He kept a notebook in which he detailed plans for future birding excursions, and in his precise handwriting he filled in three pages for our roseate tern trip.

And then, last year, when I'd asked Dad what he wanted and his answer had been vague, I'd remembered. "The roseate terns," I'd said. I'd found that notebook with the plans we'd made that long ago fall day and read them out to him. Things have changed since then, not least the designation of protected areas, but Dad's name still carries weight in the birding world so here we are, in June, Dad and I on our way to North Brother island.

But here, now, I am alone. Everyone else has moved to the other side of the boat to photograph the porpoises which are following us out of the harbour but I can't let go of the rail; gripping it feels like the best way to ward off the vomit I can already taste in the back of my throat.

The deckhand does double duty as our tour guide, his voice crackling over an old PA system, giving a brief history of the geology of the islands we're passing, basic information about puffins, telling us to look out for harbour seals.

Two young girls and their father cross the deck and stand next to me at the railing, the girls' excited chatter punctuated with likes and you knows. They soon lose interest in the view of the scrubby forest and wind turbines and go off in search of something, like, more exciting, leaving only their father and I. I look at him (roughly my age, he looks as ill as I feel) then at his hands, which are holding tight to the rail. Farmer's hands with big fingers, rough skin, short nails. A kink in the baby finger on his left hand. Like Dad's. I look back at his face.

This habit of mine, staring at strangers. Staring, and wondering. Could this man be my brother, Daniel? I look at the man's profile again and he makes eye contact.

"Rough," he says, dipping his chin towards the whitecaps.

I nod. This is the tail end of a storm which wound its way up from the Caribbean and ours is the first trip out in ten days. I assumed the Captain was joking when he told us to get ready for fifteen-foot waves. Apparently not. I could have paid more attention to the weather report, but this is the right week to come. This was the original plan. The eggs, laid in late May, will now be hatching. Two, most likely, though chances are only one will survive. That will be considered a breeding success, if one baby survives to become a fledgling.

There's an entire chapter in Dad's book devoted to common ornithological terms. Semi-precocial, pullus, fledgling - last night in the bed and breakfast, a farmhouse with wraparound porch and flaking white paint - I chanted them from a to z, mentally ticking all the ones that apply to today's terns. I can feel the book in my inside breast pocket, the binoculars around my neck squishing it to my chest. As a child I loved checking off the birds I'd seen, keeping lists from the Christmas Day count, the summer holidays, our canoe trips. And I loved most of all the pre-dawn

Notes towards Recovery

walks with Dad when we met other birders with Dad's book in their hands. I embarrassed him, always, when I told them he'd sign it for them. His is one of the definitive guides to birds of northeastern Ontario, right up there with Peterson and Sibley. A boater with Daniel, a birder with me.

"Twitcher?" my rail mate guesses. "Here for the puffins?"

"Terns," I say. And at his blank look, "Like seagulls." Which is almost true. Families Sternidae and Laridae are closely related.

He gives me a weak smile. "You're enduring this foul weather for some shithawks? Hope it's worth it." A big wave, the boat lifts and slaps down onto the sea, making him gag and lower his head over the rail.

This man is not my brother. Little as he ever cared about our hobby (obsession, Daniel called it), he would never refer to gulls as shithawks. At first glance it was possible. But that's the thing. It's always possible. When I can't sleep I watch family dramas where a shift in the music signals a quarter of an hour until the credits. Just long enough for two estranged siblings, sisters most likely, to meet in some extraordinary place and explain, forgive, reunite. A collage of snapshots showing them as they were in the past and as they will be in the future. All forgiven. Best friends again.

I know how it goes. I also know that if I am ever to see my brother again it's unlikely to be on a boat tour off the coast of Nova Scotia. I have imagined moments, conversations, envisioned how it might feel to offer an olive branch, practiced a smile. Wonder if I'd turn and walk away, as he did the last time I saw him. In the local grocery store, pushing a full cart which he abandoned in the dried goods aisle. I didn't even manage a hello because he'd spotted me first. It was late Saturday afternoon before that Thanksgiving Monday. I looked into his cart but there were no clues about his life, just a turkey, cranberries, tinned pumpkin. Exactly what you'd expect, exactly what I was buying.

Later, days later, I realized the correct, the kind thing to do, would have been to buy my brother's groceries and have someone deliver them to him, someone who knew where he was staying. Shops in our hometown still close on Sunday so he would have gone without the traditional meal. But I didn't think of that in time. Instead I paid for my shopping, drove to my parents' house, and made the sage and onion stuffing and the pumpkin pie and the maple-glazed squash for my mother's last Thanksgiving meal. I chopped a lot of onions to explain away my tears and debated with myself whether it would be more thoughtful to report the sighting or not. I wondered who Daniel was visiting, what friends of his remained in town, what sort of person could see his sister and walk away like that, not visit his dying mother. In the end I said nothing; I couldn't stand the thought of the hurt in my mother's eyes.

The doctors had named the disease, explained why parts of her atria were no longer working as they should, but I knew better. More than one ornithologist has suggested that the birds who mate for life, turtle doves, swans, snow geese, can die of a broken heart if they lose a child.

The deckhand's commentary continues: leatherback turtles, whales, the cod fishing industry. A mention of my pink-breasted terns, their distinctive two-note call, the likelihood of only one of the two babies surviving to adulthood. They are accustomed to a certain amount of loss, says the deckhand, as if he knows this, as if he's spoken to the birds and they've reassured him, it's all right, we're accustomed to this.

I turn to the man at my side and start to tell him more. Roseates are an old species, I explain. They breed in colonies close to, but estranged from other terns. They take, or are given,

Notes towards Recovery

the less favourable nesting areas and create a scrape in the sand or gravel which they cushion with softer reeds and grasses. His daughters interrupt us, rushing back in mid-argument about whose turn it is to use the iPhone. He mediates, sends them off, shrugs at me. "Siblings."

I thought it might be one good thing I could do for Dad, finding Daniel. For myself, I wasn't sure that seeing him again would restore the part of me I'd lost when he left. The days of skating on the river, summer camping holidays, secrets in our treehouse - so long ago. And even farther back, the nights we'd snuggled on the sofa to listen to Dad's bedtime stories which always started the same way: "When I was a little boy in Nova Scotia." Until we could recite them, word for word, and I had a clear picture in my mind of the boy who bullied him in fifth grade, the one Dad had raced and beaten to the forest for the best Christmas tree. The smell of the hogs his parents raised, the taste of his mother's apple brown betty. The vignettes from Dad's childhood had been one of the anchors in our childhood. Or, at any rate, mine.

My brother had made clear his choice. I wrote to him, two letters, years apart, both returned with a 'not at this address' message, scribbled over the front of one, stamped over the other. His handwriting, perhaps, or that of a new tenant in the apartment building, new home owner? I didn't know if it was true, no longer at this address, or his way of declaring that nothing had changed. As stubborn and as proud as he'd always been. So like our parents. "No contact! No contact ever!" was the last thing he'd yelled at me the day he left.

Last year I tried online, typing his name into Google, LinkedIn, Facebook and several of those websites that promise to find anyone anywhere, for the low low price of. I paid. I read random obits in case he'd predeceased us both. I called his childhood friends. It was only when I seriously considered hiring a private investigator that I told myself I had to stop searching. For Daniel, for the real reason he'd left the family, for any hope of truly understanding how an argument about a career choice could lead to estrangement. Instead I gathered maps and books and sat with Dad and planned this holiday for the two of us.

The puffin island comes into sight and there's a Parks Canada man waiting in a Boston Whaler. I thank the captain, say goodbye to the man with the kinked baby finger, and make my way across the gunwale of the big boat to clamber down into the shallow dinghy.

Once we've set off, I raise Dad's binoculars to my eyes, scanning the sky, focusing in on the birds that are catching the wind and diving for fish. Black guillemots, great black-backed gulls, eiders, and - there - our terns. Their long tail feathers and blush pink breeding colours as elegant as Audubon promised. As we near the rocky shore the Parks Canada man cuts the motor and points out the scrapes where the eggs and days-old hatchlings are.

In January we visited the doctor's office, the same doctor who'd given us the best-case scenario of three months for Mum. I'd panicked. "I can't lose you too, I can't let go. I don't know how to." I had clung to my Dad's arm like a selfish child and added, it's not fair, I can't do this again, you can't leave me alone.

Dad had patted my hand, held it tight against his arm. "You'll be OK Daisy-girl," he'd said, using a nickname I'd not heard in years. "You know how to cope. You'll figure out what to do." That was the evening I found his notes about this trip, read them aloud to him, got down the same maps and books we'd looked at with Mum.

41

Notes towards Recovery

I don't believe the deckhand's version is correct. I don't believe a tern becomes accustomed to a certain amount of loss. She must hope, every year when she lays two eggs, she must think: maybe this is the year both my children will thrive.

I take the mulberry bark envelope from my inside pocket where it's nestled against Dad's book, and lean over the edge of the whaler, holding it close to the water, opening one end. I've been warned this won't be romantic, a gentle breeze won't pick up the ash and carry some of it to the heavens, sprinkling the rest on the surface of the sea, sparkling in a ray of sunshine which breaks through a grey cloud, illuminating a clear path ahead. But this envelope, this urn, is supposed to help the process, float for a few moments before gracefully submerging.

There is none of that. A stickiness and a sinking and then a wave snatches it, leaving only a dark smudge on my hand which is rinsed away by the next wave. The poem I start to recite is drowned out by the harsh call of a tern. A few feet away there is a reply from another.

Grafting

You understand trees; Mum thinks you can speak to them. She used to tell me, often, of the wild land next to your grandfather's farm in Nova Scotia where, as a teenager, you discovered an orchard so many years abandoned that your grandfather recalled only his eldest brother gathering windfalls for the pigs. She describes how you cared for that orchard over the course of three summers, pruning, splicing and grafting, bringing those trees back to fruit-bearing life.

She remembers the summer before the land was sold, when she was heavily pregnant with me, spending hours in the kitchen. You brought her apples and the two of you baked pies and crumbles and tea cakes and canned applesauce until every jar in the pantry was full. All the middle sisters must have helped too, but that's not the only time Mum has left them out of a story, making it just about the two of you. Sometimes she grows melancholy and regrets not buying those acres for you. But she was the eldest, the sensible one, and she couldn't have imagined borrowing money from the bank, not for a parcel of scrubland, not when she and Dad were so broke themselves.

There are photos from the following spring of a fat baby lying on a picnic blanket under one of your favourite trees, laughing

Notes towards Recovery

up into a shower of blossoms. You're leaning over me, tickling my belly, probably cooing that you are my Aunt Hazlenut (this is the name I have called you from the time I could speak). I believe my mother's expression holds the merest hint of jealousy, but maybe that's just the way the shadow falls across her face.

Throughout my childhood, if the phone rang at three in the morning, I knew it was you. Time has never been something you cared much about, except on New Year's Eve. The year I was six you took me skating on the lake on the last day of December. You'd spent all day shovelling a rink, and then you built a bonfire on the shore. You had little pots of chemicals and when we'd had enough skating we tossed them into the flames to make coloured sparks. Make a wish, you said, so I did, and then I asked you what your wish was. You didn't answer the question but told me how you loved this annual midnight. "Fresh start. The chance to resign." You said it twice and I got that it was a trick word, and knew you were signing up again, not quitting. Then you pulled a bottle of sparkling grape juice from a snowbank and taught me the words to Old Lang Syne. I thought we were drinking champagne and I knew I would never again see anything as magical as green and purple flames. I think of you every single New Year's Eve.

So many treats you gave me, so many wonderful memories. Like the fall I was five and couldn't decide what I wanted to be for Halloween until the night before, when I chose Babar disguised as a dinosaur. Mum said that was impossible, I'd have to look through the dress-up box the next day and find something else. But you said nothing is ever impossible. You must have stayed up the whole night sewing. By breakfast you'd made the elephant part of the costume and when I got home at lunchtime he was dressed as a dinosaur. I was so excited I put him right on and refused to change when I went back to school or that night after the trick-or-treating. Mum scolded you for spoiling me but you only laughed, saying it was unconditional love.

When I was eight Mum and Dad told me about the baby (hadn't I always wanted a brother or sister, wouldn't this be fun?) and I panicked that you might love him or her more. "Never. Never more," you said. Your gift for my new sibling was a tiny seedling, a hazelnut tree, which you planted in the front garden. Aunt Sally's husband, Uncle Daniel, said it would never grow, we lived too far north, but you laughed and told him, "This tree will weather."

Soon after Judith was born I had to do a report on potato farming in Prince Edward Island. "I've never been to Prince Edward Island," I complained. "What do I know about their potatoes?"

You said you'd help me, and told my parents we'd be back on Sunday, that you'd give them time alone with the new baby. Then we flew down to the Maritimes. We toured the Anne of Green Gables house and ate lobsters with our fingers and knelt in that red soil to dig for potatoes. You took me to a farming museum and a fishing village and we had french fries for breakfast.

Mum was furious when we got home late Sunday night. "Where did that money come from? I bet that was your rent for the next two months." I wasn't supposed to be listening but I heard you both shouting in the kitchen, even over the screams from the baby's room.

"I guess it's my money, Rebecca." (I'd never heard you call Mum by her full name before. She was always Becky, Becks or Bee.) "If I want to eat cheap pasta for two months in exchange for a weekend with my niece, then that's my choice." The door slammed so hard the house shook, and the baby screamed even louder and I hated you both for ruining everything and when I

Notes towards Recovery

got my report back, A+ circled in red on the cover page, I didn't even show you.

For a long time after that the highchair was in the place where your chair should have been.

It was Dad, sitting on the side of my bed one evening, who told me you were in hospital. I sat up, demanded to be taken to see you. Again Mum was angry, she said I was too young. But Dad disagreed and in the end we all went, even the baby.

You didn't look sick. You were wearing pyjamas, curled up on a bed, the way I'd seen you curled up on a sofa many times before. But you didn't look at me, not even when I squeezed your hand and told you I loved you. I watched tears roll down the side of your nose and plop onto the thin white pillow.

"You shouldn't have brought her," you said to my parents. "I didn't want her to see me like this. I only ever want you all to see me on good days."

My Mum's voice held the same softness she used with Judith. "That's not your choice," she said. "We love you on your good days and we love you on your less good days." Then she started crying too, and Dad took the baby and I out of the room and down to the hospital cafeteria where he let me eat two slices of fake chocolate cake, layered with fake icing. He explained about your sickness, the manic times when you were full of energy and didn't sleep and the sad times when you needed to sleep all the time. About how it was tough, sometimes, for you to make good decisions and that it was his and Mum's job to help you even when you found it very difficult to ask for help. Some people get stuck with bad eyesight or a heart that doesn't work very well, he explained, but your poor aunt got stuck with this.

I kept shoving cake into my mouth and tried not to listen to what he was saying. You were my favourite, I didn't want you to be sick. I didn't want all our expeditions to have been a manic phase. I didn't want you to have to stay in this sickly lemon-scented building and I didn't want you to joke about being nuttier than a fruitcake, that's why you were Hazel Nut. In the car on the way home I vomited up all the cake.

Judy's Christening was postponed until you came out of hospital and then Mum threw an enormous party, inviting all the other aunts and uncles to come and stay with us. After the church service and the formal reception were over we sat round the table and the sisters talked about their childhood. Sally driving the car through the garage door. The time the raccoon broke into the kitchen. We all laughed. But you were the one who told the best and funniest stories.

"How do you remember that?" asked Aunt Sally. "You were only four when that happened."

"I am the Keeper of the Stories," you said. "That is my job."

"And something to stay well for?" asked my mother. Her voice was tentative, then she passed Judy to you to hold. "There are a lot more stories to come. And these meds are working. They're working well."

You didn't reply.

We were all sent to bed at some point, myself and all the cousins on camping mattresses on the floor of Dad's study, but no one noticed when I crept out to sit on the landing at the top of the stairs, out of sight of the adults. The men were smoking cigars, a gift from Uncle Daniel, and my mother was - yet again - telling everyone about Hazel's Orchard. "You're a tree whisperer," one of the sisters said.

"I only worry when they stop whispering back to me," you said. You were the only one who laughed. "Oh for fuck's sake." I had never heard that word aloud before in this house. I waited in shocked silence. "You have to lighten up. It's my illness so I get to

47

Notes towards Recovery

joke about it. I told the head-shrinker the other day I was feeling sanguine. Get it?" You laughed again.

"Does joking help?" I think that was my father. "We all want to know what we can do to help."

You didn't answer his question. Instead you started talking about the hospital, how you were so detached from your body that you saw it from a distance. So dulled by the drugs, so sluggish that it became a coping mechanism, cutting yourself off from the pain. That's what it was about trees, you tried to explain. The rough bark, the smooth petals, the stickiness of the budding leaves, things that made you believe if you could feel something so tactile maybe there was a way back into feeling emotions as well.

Aunt Sally - I think it was Aunt Sally - said it was more than that, it had to be, watching the plants grow and flourish. Knowing that, even now, the cycle continued and every fall there were apples on those trees. That they were weathering the years. And then there was a discussion about 'weathering' - about how it meant withstanding the elements and the opposite too, being worn away by them. And my mother's offer (in my memory it is a desperate plea) to buy you a plot of land so you could grow more fruit trees.

I must have fallen asleep at some point and been found and tucked back into my sleeping bag. In the morning the house smelled of cigar smoke and sweet wine and Judy smiled at me. She'd been smiling for weeks, but this was the first time it was just for me. My baby sister. That was the moment I truly fell in love with her. My cousins and I played with her all morning, putting on a puppet show while she lay on her back smiling up at us all and in the kitchen Mum and all the Aunts washed and put away the dishes and reheated leftovers for lunch.

It has become so important a memory, that weekend sixteen years ago, because it was the last time we were all together. One aunt got a job out west. Uncle Daniel had an affair with his secretary, packed a single suitcase and left. And you left too, you moved to a commune in Madawaska, and you stopped taking your meds. Judy doesn't know you. She barely thinks of you when she's researching our family tree and I hesitate before reminding her. I'm home for a month of holiday before I start my doctorate and amazed at how poised and beautiful my baby sister has become in this last year that I've been away. In awe of this remarkable person my parents have produced and raised, I tease her about her boyfriend and she teases me back about my lack of one.

Uncle Daniel was wrong. Despite the climate and lack of knowledgeable care, Judy's tree produced for the first time the previous year and now it is again heavy with nuts. One day I make her pose for photographs, sitting under the tree on a blanket. Just because.

Dad has taken to serving drinks and snacks before dinner, joking that this is practice for his retirement, and this evening I choose that time to ask about you.

When the phone rings at three in the morning, says Mum, I always know it's your Aunt Hazel.

Judy rolls her eyes, suddenly a child. If she asks for money they always send it, she tells me, no questions, no demands. So out of character for our parents, she says, though to be fair Mum always tries to needle out an address so she can visit. Not right now, seems to be your answer, or not yet.

I ask if there is really no information beyond a post box number. Then I tell Judy the story of my A+ report and we laugh at the naughtiness of french fries for breakfast. She grows pensive. "I wish I'd known her."

Notes towards Recovery

"She's the best, my favourite of all the Aunts," I tell her, making sure to speak of you in the present tense but wondering, even as I do, if you have left instructions so we will be notified of your passing. "We should go and look for her," I say. I make a list of places we could start, communes, orchards, maybe the Niagara region. Judy, practical as our mother, adds a list of hospitals and mental health care services we should contact. Then, 'tell me about her,' she asks.

She is the Keeper of the Stories, I think, not me. But I start to talk about the orchard and the magic flames and your love of Janus words. "To splice," I say. "It can mean to join together or to cut in two."

Mirrored

I thought I'd manage without a map. I could have stayed on the Queensway with its impossible-to-miss signposted route to Ottawa airport but instead I'd turned off the highway, confident I'd be able to navigate my way along a parallel back road. And I got lost.

The farming community I'd known as a child had been paved over. Streets of houses, one indistinguishable from the next, and strip malls, and a cluster of office blocks, and apartment towers all rippled out from a stadium which appeared to be the heart of this community. It was a fluke - the wedding of a dear friend's daughter, which had brought me back to the Ottawa Valley. Before I caught my plane home I wanted to smell some freshly turned earth, hear wind through a field of corn, and buy a bag of the local cheese curds that would squeak as I ate them.

I finally left the box stores that edged the suburb and over a slight hill I saw two buildings at a dip in the road. Drove by a gas station, clearly abandoned, where I half expected to see a pop machine selling long-forgotten brands of soda for a nickel a bottle, and then a long, single-storey structure, the weathered grey of an old barn. As I went past I turned my head, and there,

Notes towards Recovery

in a dusty yard displaying a hodgepodge of old furniture, was my grandmother's mirrored washstand.

I hit the brakes, then slowed the car properly, backed up and pulled neatly to the side of the road, already parked before I was quite aware of my need to go and touch the maple washstand I hadn't thought about for more than fifty years.

'Valley Valuables' said a hand-painted sign above the store's double doors. Underneath, in smaller letters: 'We Buy Junk - We Sell Antiques! Oil lamps, Butter prints, Ceramics, Collectibles!' Heaped on wheeled pallets, the haphazard display of furniture was labelled with faded hand-written notices. I didn't stop to look at anything else - there, wedged between a grain scale 'great as a coffee table!' and a buffet 'with pie shelf!' was the washstand.

A big, boxy base on short legs with a rectangular swivelled mirror attached to the top that creaked when I pulled it square. It was functional rather than beautiful, the only ornamentation the cobalt blue glass drawer pulls. I held two of them in my hand and pulled open the top drawer, leaning over it to breathe in the musty air, imagining hints of the moth-repellant cloves, thyme and rosemary sachets Grandmother kept tucked between the dark green towels on which she'd crocheted borders of daisies.

I blew away a layer of pollen and dust from the top of the stand, to reveal the orangey-brown wood with its grainy pattern. 'So much storage space!' said the note. True. It had held all the towels as well as everyday toiletries which my grandmother believed ought to be kept out of sight and the specially hidden vanity items: a sliver-backed hairbrush and mirror set, a tube of Max Factor Rose Red lipstick and a white box called Modess.

A kid in a plaid shirt and blue jeans ambled over. "Nice dresser," he said. "Bird's eye maple, probably made right here in the Ottawa Valley. Solid. Twenty bucks." He smiled, tilted his head in a friendly way and wandered off to the far corner of the lot where he lit a cigarette, clearly his primary reason for venturing outside.

Not a dresser, a washstand, I wanted to correct him. But I could see that he was right; it was a mirrored dresser. Because it had lived in the bathroom and held basin and pitcher, I had always thought of it as a washstand. I used a tissue in my pocket to rub off a patch of grime in the middle. The washbasin and pitcher, white ceramic with a faded pattern of pale pink flowers, with a chip on the handle that could catch you if didn't pay attention, they had sat there - just there, just so.

My grandparents' bathroom was off the kitchen; not an unusual floor plan in rural Ontario back then. Water for bathing was heated on the wood stove in my father's day and the shorter the distance it had to be carried the easier. I knew from his stories that when he was a child baths were a weekly event; Saturday evenings, the night before church. St. John's, the same church our grandparents took us to worship.

The township had raised funds for a new oil furnace and that summer they were digging a basement to install it. Two men shovelled out the earth and two more brought the buckets up through a hole in the floor with a rope pulley. My sister and I were allowed to help empty the buckets, but I suspect we mostly rushed about the yard with the other children, waiting for the women to set out the fried chicken, potato salad, dills, date bread and thick wedges of watermelon. A skull was found once, various theories were offered, and then it was buried in the graveyard.

I recall little about the Sunday services themselves other than the smell of the communion bread which filled the church as it baked. Every so often I walk past a shop which purports to cook bread on the premises and am taken back to those Sunday mornings and the warm, yeasty scent I associate with prayers.

Notes towards Recovery

I daydreamed through the sermons, and often opened a single eye to peek about during the heads-down prayers. Once I met the gaze of another child, a boy with red hair and a splatter of freckles across his face. He saw me looking at him and winked, then crossed his eyes as if challenging me to laugh. I scrunched my own tight shut then, and didn't look back in his direction, ever.

The mirror swung in a breeze and I felt a rush of unrelated fragments of memory from those long-ago months. Picking broccoli and tomatoes and beans, making up the honeycomb boxes in the barn's attic, the taste of fresh milk. My morning ritual that summer: using both hands to pour water from the pitcher into the basin, then standing on my tiptoes to wet, soap, wash and rinse my face. There was running water by then, a sink similar to the one at home. But I suppose I thought it was romantic to use the old-fashioned pitcher and basin, or perhaps I was pretending to be some storybook child.

In the yard of 'Valley Valuables' I knelt and opened every drawer, in case there was something - a scrap of paper with my grandmother's confident handwriting on it, a thread from one of her green towels - imagining as I did so, my ex-husband's voice. Stop looking for things you'll never find, Miriam. But see, I silently argued. See what I've found. Our map mirror.

It was my big sister, Janet, who named it. The silver backing had peeled away from the glass in trails, leaving behind what looked to us like a map. Our grandmother bathed us together, giving us thick bright crayon soap to play with in the claw-footed tub. We played tic-tac-toe and drew Noah's Ark on the waterline and all the animals waiting to board. And one evening, as the water turned murky and started to cool Janet said she'd 'do' my face and instructed me to close my eyes. I leant towards her, squealing with delight at the smooth crayon on my wet skin, just as I imagined real make up felt. "Stay Still, Miriam. Stop moving," she ordered and I obeyed, not because of her bossy tone of voice or because I'd always been told to mind her, but because she was my best friend and I'd have done anything she asked. I could feel her drawing on my cheek and imagined it was a beauty spot like that movie star had. I guessed she was giving me a bright red lips, blue eye shadow and pink cheeks like a fairy-tale princess. I sighed with pleasure and as soon as she was finished I jumped out of the bath and skipped over to the mirror, cleaning away a bit of steam so I could see.

It wasn't a beauty spot she'd drawn on my cheek, but a tear. "Oh." I wanted to love what she'd done. "But you gave me a clown face," I said, and reached up to mark a big X across my reflection in the mirror.

'X marks the spot,' said Janet.

Suddenly we'd discovered a treasure map, and my clown face was forgotten. For the remainder of the summer we worked to decipher our map mirror and translate its message into buried treasure hidden somewhere on the farm.

The farm's real treasures were the heirloom potatoes my grandfather grew. No potato, not from St. Lawrence Market or the best organic grocery store in Vancouver, or the top restaurants I've eaten at around the world has ever tasted as rich and creamy as the ones I took for granted that summer. My grandmother served potatoes at every meal, like meat and milk they were considered a necessity rather than a side dish. Roasted, boiled, mashed with butter and the creamy milk we drank. (Skim milk, then, was feed for pigs and chickens.) There'd be a roast with gravy and stuffing, biscuits, and bright green beans served glistening with butter and more cream, salt and pepper. That's the taste I return to when

Notes towards Recovery

I want to recapture my childhood, although I don't recall my mother ever serving us beans in the same way.

And we were allowed to dig for potatoes whenever we wanted, just as we were allowed to roam about all day, explore as we wished and even go paddling in the stream by ourselves. A thousand miles from Toronto, where I had to look both ways, beware of the street cars, and hold my mother's hand to cross the street. There was no sound of traffic, just the tractor, the chickens, and some afternoons the sharp snap of each downy green bean as we topped and tailed a milk pail full of them, sitting around the kitchen table, my grandmother, my sister and I.

"Tell me about the day my Daddy was born on this table," I often said.

My grandmother would look at me, stern, though not unsmiling, above her cats-eyes glasses.

"Please," I'd add. The magic word. Years later, when I raised my own daughters and tried to teach them basic manners, I'd ask: What's the magic word? and it worked just as well.

That was my favourite of all the stories, and my grandmother told it well. First she'd run her hand across the pitted pine, as if smoothing away the wrinkles from a sheet when she made the big double bed my sister and I shared. "Your Grandpa was out in the barn taking care of the morning chores and I was fixing breakfast. I'd known that your father was due, but I thought he might wait a few more days. When he made it known he was ready, right then, I called your Grandpa, who came in saying that whatever it was had better be important because he still had five cows to milk." She'd smile then and pick up a handful of beans, breaking off the ends - snap, snap.

"I told him what was happening and he picked up the telephone and shouted for a woman, any woman, to come and help." I knew how he did this: my sister and I had memorised all the different ring combinations of the party line telephone, knew which one belonged to which neighbour. "Soon enough Mrs. Lowell rushed in. She set to boiling water and she told me to clear off the breakfast dishes and lie down on the table. And by the time your Grandpa came back from milking those last five cows he had a son."

I'd run my hand over the wooden table then. "And that's how Daddy was born." I loved that story, both that version and the one our grandfather told us, in which the cows all knew something was up and as a result they were slow and disagreeable that morning. Not only did the milking take twice the usual time, but when he got back to the kitchen Mrs. Lowell shooed him out of the way to go and milk the cows in her barn that she'd had to abandon. But not before she passed him the baby that would be his only child.

"And?" I'd prompt both grandparents.

"And Mrs. Lowell took one look at your father and told us, my you'll be proud of that one."

And they were, I knew. There was a wall of photographs of my Daddy, and several of Janet and I. None of Mummy save for a single wedding portrait, but I never asked why.

The farm machinery, the animals, my grandparents' voices. And the rain that kept us cooped up indoors for days in a row after weeks of freedom to roam about, for the second half of our summer it too became a background noise, summer-soft against the screened porch windows, but constant. It was still a working farm and every day there was still a day's worth of chores to do regardless of the weather, but it never occurred to me that two children might have been an inconvenience.

The rain continued through August; I've no idea how it affected the digging of the new church basement or the crops or the cows. The paddling stream swelled up and rapids appeared

Notes towards Recovery

where none had been. The red-haired boy tried to swim across it on a dare, and nearly paid with his life. There was a conversation on the telephone one evening between my grandmother and my parents. We were not given a chance to say hello. I overheard enough to worry that Janet and I were going to be sent back to the city because of the rain. As it turned out, my father asked his parents to keep us for the final two weeks of summer as well; the originally promised family summer holiday was not going to take place as planned after all. It was several years before I made the connection between our having been sent away that summer and my father's leaving our mother. His floozy, my sister called his new wife, refusing ever to visit them at his new house, refusing ever to have anything to do with our baby stepbrother when he arrived. My poor mother; at the time I only thought how pleased she must have been to start a job that meant wearing high heeled shoes, jackets that matched her skirts, and lipstick every day.

The sun must have come out again, and my sister and I must have resumed our carefree exploration of the farmland and forest, picking blueberries, digging for potatoes, racing up and down the elm-lined driveway looking for treasure.

"We can re-silver that mirror for you. And arrange shipping." The voice of the kid, back from his cigarette break, pulled me back into the dusty yard. Shipping. I must have looked like a tourist, not from here, or else he'd noticed the rental sticker on the car.

"Do you know where it came from?" I asked.

He shrugged. "One of those houses that got torn down for a new subdivision." He nodded his chin in the direction I'd been heading. "Some old lady asked us to clear out her house."

An old lady. But .. even before I finished the thought that my grandmother, my mother, were no longer alive, I realized that to this kid I was also, no doubt, an 'old' lady. Had Janet lived, been standing beside me, he'd not have been able to guess who was the older of the two of us. As eldest grandchild she might have inherited the house; I thought of her topping and tailing beans, digging potatoes, and felt a rush of comfort imagining her living in that place where we'd both been so happy. I never knew what happened to the farmhouse after my grandparents died. I grew up, moved out west, got married and raised my own two daughters, naming one after the aunt she never got a chance to meet. I heard the farmland had been sold to commercial potato producers who grew for Schnieders, later Hostess, later Lay's, for their chips. I always bought that brand of potato chips in case the potatoes came from The Elms' land, and once refused to eat from a different brand of potato chips my husband picked up. A ridiculous argument, like so many of them.

I looked down at my hands, still playing with the drawer pulls. Thick blue veins showed through wrinkled skin marked with faded age spots and I blinked and saw my chubby little-girl hands, playing… with painted ceramic pulls, not glass. And remembered three smaller drawers across the top, and a darker stain on the wood. This wasn't my grandmother's washstand after all.

"I knew a farm like that," I said, patting the dresser one last time. "I wish I could take this but I live in a tiny apartment." I smiled. "Thank you." And I drove off before he could see the old-lady tears that were gathering in the corners of my eyes.

Three miles on I passed a brown stone church, on a street of triple-garaged homes, no sign of red brick farmhouses and land divided by split-rail fences. A subdivision named The Elms was the only remnant of the farm I could find. See? I told my ex-husband in our imaginary conversation. See, I wasn't lost after all.

Notes towards Recovery

I glanced at my watch as if to justify my choice not to stop or even linger, as if catching the plane back to my empty apartment was more important than touring the basement of St John's church. It was a benchmark of my childhood, that summer, and the holiday by which I'd judged all others since and yet it occurred to me that I had never once told my husband about it. I sped by rows of cul-de-sacs and more of the cookie-cutter houses, and a general store whose window advertised local artwork and maple walnut fudge, and a one room schoolhouse turned into museum. 'Step back in time - see how we lived a lifetime ago.' I shook my head as I drove on, arguing that it wasn't a lifetime ago, it was my lifetime. Mine.

What was the washstand to my grandmother, I wondered, a family heirloom or just a useful piece of furniture? And what about the impostor that I'd wasted half an hour looking at. Had I paid the twenty dollars asked, would I have been buying a piece of junk or an antique?

How had I thought for a moment it was my grandmother's washstand? I shook my head. It must have been the sun's glare, making me think I could see a map on the mirror where there was none. Almost all the silver backing had peeled off, so much that I hadn't even been able to make out my own reflection.

Moon Jellies

I could have said no. Richard was away on one of his business trips, delayed by the threat of an early summer hurricane working its way up the east coast when he called to remind me we were due to collect his grandmother from the airport and look after her for the day.

I could have booked an airport limo service to meet her and deliver her to his parents' house, the oversized home in the suburbs with its four-car garage, but I was introvert, not unfriendly. I reminded him that I'd never met her.

Hold up a sign, he said. Her name is Marit Smid.

That wasn't what I'd meant. I knew that much about his grandmother. When she immigrated to Alberta from the Netherlands after the war, her only son, Matthijs Smid, became Matthew Smith because, he said, she wanted him to be Canadian. She herself had never changed her name, nor ever moved away from Lethbridge. Every year Matthew asked her to come live in Ontario and every year she refused.

"Take her out to lunch then drop her at my folks' place. She'll be tired, she can have a rest until they get home from work."

"Where should we go for lunch? What does she like?"

Notes towards Recovery

Silence. I imagined him rolling his eyes. "I don't know," he said. "Anywhere. It doesn't matter. She's an old lady, not like your grandmothers."

This is what I knew of grandmothers: one was a farmer's daughter, capable of fixing tractors and sewing curtains, an excellent cook, she spoke of the boom and bust of the mining industry, swore in French and treated both my grandfather and my father as if they were twelve years old and in need of constant supervision. The other was American, wore blue jeans, dyed her permed hair blonde, drank beer from a bottle and arrived every summer of my childhood with a suitcase full of presents my mother deemed inappropriate. Richard had met them both, but was not interested much in families, which maybe explained why I had never met his grandmother.

About airports I knew far less. For the first fifteen years or so of my life my family left town four times a year. We spent Thanksgiving long weekend with my paternal grandparents up in Elliot Lake, went down to Toronto in mid-December for a weekend of Christmas Shopping and the Nutcracker Ballet. At the start of the summer - those brief weeks when the mosquitoes have died off but it's not yet stinking hot - we went camping for seven days, and at the end of August we went on a two-week road trip. Every year somewhere else - the Eastern Townships, the Maritimes, New England, and the year I turned twelve, all the way out to Vancouver.

My father worked for the government all his life, and never took more than three weeks' holiday a year, not even when he'd put in enough time, rising up the scale, to merit a full five.

What can a child guess? Everything our family did was the only normal I knew. In the small town where we lived most people took similar holidays, for sure everyone camped. Some people spent the winter school break skiing or lying on a beach somewhere warm but I couldn't imagine flying; what I knew was driving.

Mother made picnics to eat in the car - big enough for days' worth of meals. Sandwiches of home-made bread, thick slices stuffed with baked ham and mustard, grilled beef and horseradish, and my favourite, roast chicken with mayonnaise. Meat pies cut into great wedges. Bags of carrots and radishes pulled from the garden, zucchini sticks, raw broccoli and tiny tomatoes that my brother squirted at me through his missing front teeth. Apple slices which we were allowed to dip into cinnamon sugar. And a five gallon jug of lemonade, frozen overnight so that it was icy cold for hours into the first afternoon, warm and sickly and tasting a little of plastic for the rest of the trip.

Dad liked to get an early start and stay on the road until we reached our day's destination and he'd mutter under his breath at times, "keep moving, keep moving." I longed to stop at the new McDonald's drive-through, with its bright yellow and red plastic, especially in the States when it became a drive-thru, or the neon-lit place where you rolled down your car windows and your food was brought out to you by a girl wearing roller skates and given to you on a tray that attached to your door.

After I left Richard I adopted my father's mantra as my own, hearing his voice when I reminded myself to keep moving, keep moving. By then, I understood the fear of not being able to start again if I ever stopped and wondered if I should blame my parents for not teaching me how to have a healthy argument.

They argued once a year, when we got lost in the city. As a teenager I listened for complaints about money, my brother's low grades, my poor choice in boyfriends, the things my friends' parents shouted about, but if those discussions took place in our house, I never heard them. Only ever in the car, only ever in the city.

Notes towards Recovery

It seemed every time Dad entered the city it was along a different road, an unknown route, a new way to get lost in the dark, narrow one-way system.

"Turn here," Mum would tell my father.

"Where?"

"There. There! You've missed it. Turn back."

"How?"

"I don't know! Make a U-turn!" she'd shout.

"I can't make a U-turn. This is a one-way street, Dorothy."

"We're only going one way, Francis. The wrong way."

Once, that had been a joke.

As soon as my parents, Frank and Dot, became Francis and Dorothy, my brother and I squished ourselves as far back into the station wagon's seat as possible, and looked away from each other. Even as a child I sensed it was never about driving in the city, it was never about the one-way system. The overtime, the cost of my braces, the neglected yard work. We all had to endure that hour of stress to truly appreciate the holiday that followed, which, as far as I recall, we always did.

I fell in love with Richard when, during our second year at university, he suggested we join a group of his friends flying down to Florida for reading week. I was speechless at the extravagance of the proposal because when I told him there was no way I could afford such a holiday he said he'd pay. Once it was booked I splurged on a new bikini, a pair of sunglasses and a manicure and tried not to act too excited about the prospect of my first airplane ride in front of my fellow students, for whom flying was no big deal. Cheaper, they said, and so much faster than driving down that we'd have an extra two days there.

We left the dregs of a Toronto winter, with piles of muddy snow heaped at the back of every parking lot and the wind off the lake still bitter as it whipped up Yonge Street. Stepping off the plane a few hours later there was a wall of heat, and sunshine so bright I had to close my eyes. It was magical then, and the memory of that moment still is. In a bid to recapture that extraordinary sensation I sometimes book long haul-flights; leaving Toronto at night so that I can wake up to a new climate in a different time zone.

The giddy joy of that holiday was enough to carry our relationship through the next two years, and then we moved in together. I continued on at school, working towards a doctorate in Anthropology, while Richard took a sales job that involved frequent travel across North America. To be fair to him, I don't think he realized how little money I had; we didn't discuss the imbalance in our incomes, and I was too proud to suggest a joint bank account.

So when he said over the phone, so casually, take her out to lunch, I said sure, and I took down her flight details and ironed my pale yellow sundress and cleaned the car and then, just in case, the tiny house we rented behind Eglinton bus station. I checked the weather report and thought about restaurants with back patios or roof gardens and wondered how I could ask Richard to reimburse me for a meal I couldn't afford. Then I rang my brother for advice, asking him what I could talk about with an elderly woman I didn't know.

"Meeting the grandmother, huh? Must be serious," he teased.

I hadn't yet told him of Richard's marriage proposal, or my acceptance. (The two men I loved most in the world had little in common; I'd discovered that infrequent dinners with lots of alcohol was the best way to merge my past and my future.) "Yeah," I said, and changed the subject.

I gave up trying to find a suitable, affordable restaurant and instead made and packed with care a picnic my mother would

Notes towards Recovery

have recognized. I studied the map carefully, compiling notes about parks between the airport and Richard's parents' house and I made a big sign to hold. Planning for the possibility of a road closure or early flight arrival, I left the house an hour early. What I didn't plan for was the thunderstorm that shut down the airport for an hour and fifty minutes. Maybe, I thought, Richard's storm was real. According to the woman at the gate, the plane had landed but it hadn't pulled into the designated unloading space, so the passengers had to wait.

When they finally came through the doors, every traveller looked old, tired, and slightly discombobulated. A thin white-haired woman wearing a cotton skirt and cornflower blue blouse approached me with a smile. "You must be Richard's fiancée," she said. It was the first time I'd heard myself described as such and I was startled at the unease I felt at her use of the word. This stranger knew something I'd not yet told my brother. "It's so kind of you to meet me. I could have taken a taxi cab."

"Nonsense," I said, reaching to shake her hand, realizing too late that I was still holding the sign. "You're family. Richard's parents are so sorry they couldn't meet your flight. And Richard too, naturally." I took her bag and led the way to the car.

I asked after the flight, the weather out west, made small talk until I had manoeuvred our way out of the parking lot. Then I turned to her with what I hoped was a friendly smile. "If the sun comes out-" I said. "I've made us a picnic for lunch."

"What a treat," she said. "Home-cooked food instead of an overpriced restaurant with a menu I can't decipher." I loved her from that moment on. She asked about my studies and my career options and really listened to my answers so I found myself speaking carefully rather than tossing off my usual replies. It was only when I saw an exit for Morningside Avenue that I realized I'd missed the 404 turn-off. I swerved the car across two lanes, admitted my mistake, and told her I was my mother's daughter. That made her laugh. "So, we have an adventure."

There was a sign for the zoo, so I took it. When I stopped the car the windshield wipers thudded off and I peered through the rain. "We'll have to have an indoors picnic. I think there's a lunchroom for school groups. If you don't mind-?"

"I am very content."

Content. Not happy, but content. I wondered if that was a deliberate word choice, or a transliteration from Dutch. "Please," I said, as I used most of my cash to buy one student and one senior ticket at the entrance gate. "Tell me about your life in Alberta. I know so little about you."

She shook her head. "Not so interesting. Let me tell you about Richard when he was a young boy." And we made our way to the end of a long pine table where we could sit across from each other, in a room filled with the noise of excited children who traded their treats back and forth, a cookie for a fruit roll-up, grape juice for a soda pop, a chocolate bar for a bag of potato chips.

"Squirties!" said the little boy sitting next to me when I unpacked the cherry tomatoes. "I love squirties."

"I grew them in my garden." I offered him the punnet.

He looked downcast. "I don't have anything to trade in return."

Mrs. Smid ("please, call me Marit") leaned across the table. "You could trade a piece of information," she said. "What's the number one best exhibit we should go and see?"

The boy looked serious as he considered her question and ignored all his friends who were yelling out the polar bears, the lions, the baby giraffes. "The fish," he said, before taking a handful of the tomatoes.

Notes towards Recovery

She thanked him for the advice, and looked at me. "What fun." I chose to believe she meant it all - the picnic, the children, the zoo. I sent a silent thank you to my mother for teaching me how to make a picnic. And after our lunch we made our way to the aquarium. She petted the stingrays, we watched an octopus, and we looked at every tank of fish. At the mouth to a narrower hall she paused, and then read out the sign. "Invertebrates." And I held her arm and helped her down the steps, waiting until I was sure her eyes had adjusted to the dark.

A series of black back-lit tanks held neon-coloured anemones, clams, and corals. We admired the bright jewel tones, the odd shapes. In front of the next display she stumbled, stopped. I steadied her, then looked at the sign: Aurelia aurita.

About five dozen of them, the jellyfish were the pale colour of the moon just before dawn, when the world is still black and white. Drifting up towards the surface then gliding down to the bottom of the tank, like fallen poplar leaves caught in the gentlest breeze. I was fascinated; it was only when I heard the older woman slowly release her breath that I remembered she was there, and in the dim light saw tears at the corner of her eyes.

"You're sad," I said. I took her hands in mine. "And cold." We were both dressed for a warm summer day, not an air-conditioned building. I led her to the coffee shop, sat her at a table, and then I unfolded my emergency ten dollar bill from the secret compartment of my purse and bought the fanciest coffees they sold. It's difficult now to remember what a rarity a cappuccino was back then with its frothed milk and sprinkle of cinnamon.

When I carried the drinks back to the table she was dabbing at her eyes with a cotton handkerchief. "You must forgive me," she said.

There was nothing to forgive, I assured her. I was so pleased to have had this time to meet her before next summer's wedding, and I wondered if she'd be back to visit before then, at Christmas perhaps.

She shook her head. Soft, sincere, straightforward, she told me she had come to say goodbye to her son, her daughter-in-law and her grandchildren. It was cancer, and she was grateful to have been diagnosed in time to make this last trip east.

It was my turn to grow silent then, and because it felt there could no longer be any secrets between us, I asked her what the moon jellies meant to her.

There was no way I could leave her by herself at Richard's parents' house when we left the zoo, so we went back to our tiny house; the sun reappeared and I wiped off the lawn chairs so we could sit in the garden. I made a pot of tea and took it outside, where she was kneeling by the flowers, plucking off the deadheads.

"I'm always forgetting to do that," I said, crouching down beside her.

"I do just a few of mine every time I walk by. And then I throw them," she said, scattering them across the lawn. "You never know; sometimes flowers bloom unexpectedly."

Richard called that night, when I was back at home, having safely delivered Marit to his parents. He'd be back the next afternoon, he said. He didn't ask me how the day had gone, how his grandmother was and there was no mention of the storm, whether or not it had hit.

"You were wrong," I said, as we were about to hang up.

"What?"

"You said your grandmother was old. Frail. Weak. She's the strongest woman I've ever met."

I never shared the details of that afternoon with him, yet I always blamed him for not knowing. The colleague he was sleeping

Notes towards Recovery

with was a convenient reason to call off the wedding, but if his grandmother had lived I might have gone through with it.

She was twenty-nine in September nineteen forty-four. "You have heard of Operation Market Garden," she said. "Perhaps you have seen the photographs of the American parachutists." (Had I? I wasn't sure. The next morning I went to the university library and stared at Robert Capa's photographs of the Second World War and read about Nijmegen and the revenge the locals took on the *moffenmeiden*, the women they believed guilty of sleeping with Germans. Then, sitting in a study carrel I burst into tears - noisy, snotty sobs, which I had to wipe away with scraps of paper torn from my notebook.)

"When I saw through the mist, the dawn sky full of parachutes, I believed they were coming to save us. It was a beautiful moment, that moment of hope."

I'd stirred a packet of brown sugar into the froth on the top of my coffee and waited.

"The war had taken everything," she said. "My father, our house, everything we owned. My mother needed food, a blanket. I did what I could." Another pause. "And then I did what I had to do."

First for her mother.

Then for her son.

She reached into her own handbag's secret compartment and took out a black and white photograph, smoothing a dog-eared corner before passing it to me. "Here is my baby Thijs, Richard's father."

I might have gasped, or maybe I bit my tongue. I was angry that Richard wasn't beside me, to witness this; he should have known what his grandmother endured to ensure his father's future. Matthew Smith, this baby, the man who overheated his house through the winter, saying as a child he'd never been properly warm.

She must have had a mantra, a stubborn streak, pride - something to help her put one foot in front the other as she walked through the jeering crowd that parted for her. Keep moving, keep moving. She was carrying her bald baby in her arms, her own shaved head held high.

I think of her every time I pull deadheads, a few when I walk by, and scatter them across the lawn. And, though I rarely visit aquariums, when I do, I find the moon jellies and watch them glide down through the water like a sky full of parachutists and think of death and regret.

And then I remember the hope.

The beautiful moments of hope.

Family Tree

It was, as it turned out, my very last summer living at home and perhaps that's why I remember the wild blueberries as bigger, sweeter, than any I've seen since. There was some reason, or so my mother told me, and I guess I believed her. A wildfire seven years previously, started by the McCormack boys who were smoking dope and dropped a butt - here my mother went off on a tangent about Ellen McCormack, something she'd said to my mother at a long-ago parent teacher meeting, the upshot that it wasn't entirely surprising her boys were pot-heads, but I let that part of the story drift to one side of me; those were not boys I had any interest in. The fire took out all the other shrubs and left the acidic soil ready for jack pines and berries. And then that brief burst of spring - such a surprise - in mid-March. The snow melted and I foolishly trusted spring had truly arrived - I wore a knitted blue poncho to school three days in a row. Of course the cold came back, and more snow, and it was May before I could wear my poncho again. But those few days of warmth had been just enough to get the berries into blossom and then they saved all their energy while we all endured the longs weeks until spring proper.

Notes towards Recovery

Summer came; it aways did. Late light evenings and long, lazy afternoons, and those enormous clusters of berries, plump with juice, dragging the branches of the bushes to the ground. Acres of blue, enough for the whole township to pick, and all the neighbouring communities, the air smelled of jam and pie and crumbles. Enterprising teenagers paid their younger siblings to pick while they themselves sat behind makeshift stalls on the highway. Our town was not on the way to or from any real destinations but enough tourists still drove along, willing to stop and buy wild berries by the quart, the city folk imagining a dark shape they saw in the woods might be a moose or a bear.

Mother and I - (this was the first summer I called her mother - feeling at sixteen I had outgrown the more childish Mum, but not quite as brave as my best friend who called her own parents Betty and Jack) - Mother and I picked far beyond the main patch, by the edge of one of the lakes. No one else bothered walking the extra half mile when there was no need. A mile, by the time you'd walked there and back again to the path that took you out to the lane where you could park, but at the end of each afternoon we treated ourselves to a swim and that made the trek worthwhile.

What almost-seventeen year old would spend hours each day in the stinking hot sun with a hum of jack flies (the weather so conducive for the berries had also, alas, produced the worst batch of flies in recent memory) and her mother? I suppose I had a choice, but it never occurred to me not to go on the daily expeditions. I knew that come February, when the cold days were short and colourless, I'd have spoonfuls of jam on my breakfast toast and a second helping of pie at dinner. And perhaps I was aware, too, that graduating the following June was going to change everything.

What did we talk about? My project that summer was a family tree. I had the idea that I might be able to hand it in for a social studies project to count towards my university application package. Not so conceited as it sounds, my mother's family neatly mapped odd moments in the history of eastern Canada and I knew I could produce a strong essay by focusing on three key dates.

My great-grandfather, born in Bytown on the tenth of February 1841, lived in Upper Canada for precisely one hour of his life. Then Upper Canada became Ontario, and not quite fourteen years later Bytown became Ottawa. I loved this story; it was remarkable to me that someone could be born in a place, stay always, and die somewhere different, and made Canada feel as exotic as a small foreign country with shifting borders.

He had not, in fact, stayed always but left Ottawa to manage a hotel in Saint John and that was where he met his wife who gave birth to their first son on the twentieth of June 1877, hours before their hotel burnt down in the Great Fire. Two hundred acres in nine hours. In my essay I would write that it changed the destiny of Saint John forever, offering proof enough to convince my teacher that I could, at least, set out an academic essay with argument and supporting evidence. I gilded the lily when I then tried to draw a comparison between the fire's reach over the water to passages from both Shakespeare and the Bible and my teacher remarked with red ink in the margin that I might be better served by keeping to the facts.

That child, my grandfather, ended up living in a settlement on the Ontario-Quebec border during the 1920s gold rush, and was still there in 1935 managing a mine when my mother was born. First of November. Same day as the Témiscamingue earthquake. Many times I had done the math on my fingers; he was fifty-eight years old when my mother, the oldest of six children, was born. Seventy when my youngest Uncle arrived. That could happen in

Notes towards Recovery

those days, my mother always explained, leading me to wonder if she thought it hadn't happened since, couldn't happen now.

When I was a child, first piecing together these histories, I'd worried that nothing of import happened in our town on the day of my birth. I presumed my mother consoled herself with the fact I was born in the country's centennial year, but had she managed to give birth five weeks earlier so I arrived on July first, (still, then, called Dominion Day), my birth wouldn't have been such a disappointment. The day I mentioned this to my father - it was the morning of my seventh birthday I think - he laughed out loud. "Nothing of import! Nothing of import? Your birth changed my life, your birth was the most important thing to happen here. Ever." And after that I stopped agonizing quite so much.

So as we sat in the sun, swatting at horseflies and filling six-quart baskets with the berries I begged her for stories of her childhood, ones she hadn't told me before. She'd told them all up, she said, she'd have to move on to her teenage years. She thought for a while before she spoke.

When she was fifteen (significantly younger than I was now, she reminded me, as if I might have forgotten my birthday was in two weeks' time) she took a job for the summer. Babysitting, live-in, four nights of the week. She was paid well, she said, very well, in a town where there were a lot of families living on the edge of poverty.

Why so much you must wonder, she said. (Although I hadn't.) She leaned towards me and lowered her voice. No one else would take the job. They weren't Catholics.

At that I suspect I rolled my eyes. Not everyone in Quebec in the fifties was a Catholic I said. I accused her of exaggerating, and quoted my father's fictitious title for her biography: *Lies my Mother Told Me*.

My mother would have paused, tilted her head; this was how she always dealt with my sass. Perhaps not, she allowed. But the only church in town was Catholic. It was quite a drive to the United Church, further still to a Baptist place of worship. If you weren't Catholic you pretended, that was what people did on a Sunday morning. Anyhow, she said. These people were more than just not Catholic. The husband was an engineer on the Ontario Northland Railway, driving trains between Toronto and Moosonee. His wife had just given birth and the woman they called his sister-in-law, who lived with them - she too was pregnant and due in a matter of weeks. My mother looked at me. So. You see, she said.

I did not see.

The so-called sister-in-law had no husband. Never any mention of one either, so everyone guessed they knew who the father of that baby was. Two wives, she hissed, though there was no one within sight, let alone hearing distance.

"Mother!"The idea of polygamy would have shocked me. "You have a vivid imagination." (This too was something my father often said.)

"It's true." She held her hand on her heart, or close enough. "All true."

"So that's why you were paid so well? To keep that secret? Which clearly everyone in town already knew." I didn't want to dwell on the idea of one man impregnating two women. Gross.

"But wait. Why did they need you to babysit if there was the mother and her sister-in-law, or co-wife, or whatever she was? Surely two women could look after a single baby?"

"Ah. But." This was how my mother often launched into one of her longer stories. We moved a few feet to an untouched patch of bushes, and continued picking.

Notes towards Recovery

My mother explained that when she had gone to the house to be interviewed the husband had made it clear that neither woman was to be left alone with the baby. No further details were forthcoming, but the woman who did for the neighbours and also my grandmother, said there were arguments, terrible arguments from that house whenever the husband was off driving his trains. Screaming and broken plates. My grandmother had doubts about allowing her daughter to take the job, never mind she could use the help herself at home, but it was the thought of the poor wee baby suffering that made her relent. She explained to my mother how some women don't manage childbirth as well as others, that after the baby arrives they have mad thoughts. I could picture my grandmother saying this; she'd have considered mad thoughts a sign of too much money, too much free time.

Whatever.

Maybe there was some jealousy between the women, my mother thought, the one being the first to produce a child, the other being younger and prettier, blonde hair and what we called then porcelain skin. Yvonne was pale-skinned too, but in a sickly way, with dull brown hair and bad acne.

And her husband? I asked. I wanted to build a picture of these three people. Handsome, my mother said, as if that described him. Tall, strong, blue eyes. I remember thinking he looked like one of the big American movie stars, the one in the Christmas movie.

"James Stewart. It's a Wonderful Life." I prided myself on my knowledge of trivia. But my mother didn't acknowledge what I'd said. Off she went, my mother, to take up residence in one of the guest rooms in the three story house at the bend in the river. The husband met her at the end of the lane, reminding her again that she must never leave either woman alone with the baby. It must have been awkward between you and the women, I said, imaging myself in that situation. You were just a kid with no job experience-

I beg your pardon, my mother interrupted me. Straightened her back. I was the eldest of six, she said. I had five younger bothers and more experience of changing diapers and heating milk and soothing babies than either of those two women. Yvonne and Cesily. Who were both very happy to let me take over; I hardly saw them. Cesily, the pretty, pregnant one, spent her days lying on a chaise lounge on the porch, complaining about the heat. Yvonne, the new mother, barely acknowledged the baby before she went off walking every morning.

Walking where, I wanted to know. But my mother had no idea. She said she hadn't thought it her place to ask but I wondered if she hadn't cared. The baby was a girl and my mother was delighted with the dresser full of brand new dresses from the Sears Catalogue, untouched books and brand new toys. (And, I read this between the lines, few of the chores that she'd have been expected to do at home.) She washed the diapers and the little dresses and outfits and hung them on the line as the baby slept at her feet in a bassinet, and prepared simple meals - but there was no housework to do, no garden to weed, no young boys' arguments to mediate.

It would have been the perfect way to spend that summer, my mother said.

But? I asked.

The third week the heat really was unbearable. Cesily asked me to help her pull a chaise longue down to the river where she lay, dangling her hands and feet in the water. Yvonne said there was cooler shade in the forest. My mother told me to keep the baby inside, that she'd get heatstroke otherwise, so we played in the nursery and I kept her forehead fresh with a rung-out washcloth.

Notes towards Recovery

Finally the weather broke with a morning-long thunderstorm. Lightening took out a trestle bridge up north, and the husband came home a day and a half earlier than expected. His wife wasn't there when he got home and nor was Cesily and I couldn't tell him exactly where either of them was. Yvonne had set off before the storm, she must have sought shelter somewhere. And Cesily - I hadn't seen her since breakfast. The baby and I were in here, in the house. I looked out the window but it was raining by then and I couldn't see if the white and green striped lawn chair was still at the river's edge or not. I put the baby down for a nap and offered him some lunch.

It was dark by the time Yvonne came home, soaked through. Where was Cesily she asked, why hadn't anyone called the police to organize a search party for her, what was wrong with us. I heard then the screaming that had been previously mentioned, the shattering of plates, and went to calm the baby.

As soon as the police arrived, hats held in their hands, we all knew it was bad news. Death by drowning. Luckily they said, luckily her body had washed up on shore a few miles downriver instead of being carried off. So no one would have any false hopes about her survival.

I'd filled my basket, picking berries without being aware of what I was doing. This was not a story I was going to use in my family tree project but I was desperate to know the ending. And? I demanded. What happened?

My mother shook her head. It wasn't ruled a suicide and we were all thankful for that small mercy. An autopsy was performed and the results were leaked, including the news that the unborn baby was, well was-.

Ah. So not Yvonne's husband's baby then, I clarified.

No, not possibly.

And?

But that was the end of the story, my mother said. They left soon after the funeral and the house was sold. Yvonne, poor woman, blamed herself for Cesily's death, and there were rumours that she was institutionalised in Toronto. The baby must have been sent to relatives I suppose. The husband? I have no idea.

We'd both been so engrossed in the past we neither of us noticed the bears until one of them growled at us. Then more growling, the other side of us. We were between a mother and her cub.

"Run! Run! Climb a tree!" I yelled, pushing my mother in front of me. Where did that command come from? And how did we both manage? I'd never climbed a tree before, I don't even remember noticing before that there were trees so close to where we'd been sitting. But I held my mother's foot and then half-shimmied, half-shoved her up a white pine until we could reach the branches, climbing and pulling ourselves farther and farther away from the ground, until we could go no further. I looked up into my mother's face. "It'll be okay, Mum," I whispered, and patted the bit of her I could reach.

Completely the wrong thing for us to have done, of course, running, climbing a tree. But we were lucky. The mother just wanted to keep her cub safe, and didn't chase after us, climb the tree. The two of them ate all the berries we'd picked and then lay down in the sun. We were up in the tree for the best part of two hours; when the mother and cubs ambled off we waited another half hour before getting down, which proved to be just as difficult as getting up had been. Hot, scratched, bloodied, I thought we'd go straight home but my mother pulled off her t-shirt and trousers and walked into the lake. I followed her in to the deliciously soothing water and sank down to my neck. Then, thinking of Cesily, held my hands to my stomach as if I were

Notes towards Recovery

pregnant and, keeping my eyes open, slipped all the way under the water's surface.

We held hands as we walked away and I asked the question I'd been considering the whole time I was up in the tree. The father must have come home at noon or so - you said the storm was still going on and you offered him lunch. Yvonne came home much later, it was already dark you said. And neither you nor the father had done anything to look for either of the women. So what were you doing? How did you spend the afternoon?

My mother said nothing.

Then or ever.

Surfacing

"Miss? Miss, we're here."

"Oh. Right. Sorry." Brigitte looked at the meter and passed the taxi driver two tens and two toonies. "Thanks." She opened the door, hesitated.

"It's blocked off," said the driver. "Because of the demolition. You have to cross up there." He waved his hand off to the right.

"Thanks," Brigitte said again. She got out and strode off in the direction he'd pointed in case he was watching her, as if she was navigating with ease through the crowd of Torontonians whose lives she knew nothing about and who were equally oblivious to hers. Back straight, head up, walk with purpose, show no sign of being disoriented. The street was a mess of roadworks and temporary pedestrian walkways, anyone would be confused. She turned slowly, scanning the skyline. Where was the cluster of red brick towers and turrets? Until she was eight she'd assumed the Victorian building at the end of their street was a castle. When she discovered it was a hospital "for Psychiatric Maladies and Nervous Disorders" she changed her route to school. Right now it would be a useful landmark, pointing her towards her childhood neighbourhood.

Notes towards Recovery

The elementary school, only three blocks away from the house where she and her brother, Philippe, had been raised and he now lived, happily ever after, with his wife, Claire, and daughter, Madison, who went to that same school.

This was a new thing, repeating names. She shook her head to rid it of the echo and walked up the hill, past the row of new town homes, then one block over, to her niece's school.

Brigitte had booked off for the whole day but the process had been much faster than expected, so she'd called her sister-in-law. "Claire, I'm playing hooky from work and it's such a gorgeous spring day. May I take Maddy out for lunch and the afternoon?"

She had felt Claire's reluctance over the phone.

"Please?"

"I'd really prefer some advance warning, Bree. I know she's only in Grade One, but-"

"I know. I'm sorry. My plans changed at the last moment."

"Nothing too extravagant? No expensive restaurants or shows?"

"Just a picnic in the park," promised Brigitte. "And I'll have her home in time for gymnastics. When is that again, five o'clock?"

"It's skating, at five thirty, so home by four at the latest. And stay for supper yourself, stranger. Your brother and I haven't seen you in weeks. I told him there must be a new man in your life."

Brigitte had laughed. No new man, no, but dinner would be lovely. She'd have Maddy home by four. After she hung up she'd signalled a taxi and sighed. Tonight then. No more putting it off. But first, a picnic in the park.

"Auntie Brigitte!" Her niece was waiting on a tiny bench in front of the principal's office, swinging her legs and chattering to the secretary. Jumping up, she leapt onto her Aunt and threw her arms around her neck, covering her cheeks with sticky, strawberry-jam scented kisses. "Where were you? I missed you when you were gone."

"I wasn't gone, Maddy. Just super busy at work. But I've missed you too."

The girl slipped down. "Where are we going?"

"First we're going to buy some naughty treats and then we're going to High Park."

"Can we go and see the llamas and bison? And go to the adventure playground? And will you tell me the story about the horses on the lake? Please?"

"Yes, yes, and yes," said Brigitte. Already her shoulders felt lighter; this had been a good decision, the right way to spend her afternoon.

Madison skipped down the school's front steps then reached her hand up into Brigitte's and reminded her to hold on tight when they crossed the street.

I'm holding on as tight as I can. You hold on tight too.

"Is this going to be like our secret picnics, starting with dessert?"

"It sure is. That's our special tradition."

A tradition born of the day she'd bought ice cream sundaes which were already melting by the time they reached a lunch spot. Had that been a warning sign? It didn't matter. What mattered was that in the future Madison might sometimes think of her childhood 'secret picnics' with her Aunt, and the joy of eating dessert first. There was an Italian Deli en route to the park. She made sure to toss the receipt so Claire wouldn't accuse her of extravagance.

"Look at those dancing people." Maddy pointed as they entered the park.

Brigitte followed her niece's finger and saw a group of elderly women doing Tai Chi. Years ago she had taken Tai Chi classes

Notes towards Recovery

and she realized her body was already in position. Parting the wild horse's mane. White crane spreads its wings. Her body knew exactly what to do and she finished the set.

"That was neat," said her niece. "I didn't know you could do that."

It was neat. Could muscle memory extend to more than just exercise? What about vocal chords?

They walked down through the west ravine, kicking up last fall's leftover leaves as Maddy talked non-stop until they came to a spot by the pond that she declared 'perfect' for their picnic. Over butter tarts and chocolate brownies, Brigitte told her about her picnics in this same park when she and Maddy's Dad were her age.

"With Granny and Grampa, right?" Maddy said. "I was Grampa's favourite, wasn't I?"

"Oh, Honey. Grampa died a few months before you were born. But I know he would have loved you so much if he'd met you."

Madison shook her head. "I think you might be mistakened. I think he knew me when I was a baby." She nodded, her face serious.

"He knew you were on the way, and he already loved you," said Brigitte. He hadn't recognized any of them by then, but every day when Claire visited the nursing home he'd reached out to touch her belly. That was love, everyone had agreed. Maddy started telling a story about a new girl in her class, and Brigitte tried to follow it, in part to distract herself from the memory of that locked ward and her father's blank stare. He'd been comfortable, warm and well-fed for the last years of his life, but that was little comfort to Brigitte then, even less now.

"-and she has dark blue pencils with her name stamped on them. In gold!"

Make a note to buy some name-stamped pencils for Maddy for Christmas. And maybe some for herself as well? Already she found herself needing to write down everything; her bathroom mirror and kitchen cupboards were papered with bright yellow sticky notes. "Would you like pencils with your name in gold?"

"Yes please. My real name. Madison Rose." She looked up at her Aunt. 'Did you know that we don't just share a middle name? Daddy told me that Brigitte and Madison both mean the same thing. Strong." The little girl flexed her arm muscle. "I'm not that strong. I can't even lift up your scuba tank."

"One day soon you'll carry a scuba tank and a bag of gear," said Brigitte, dividing a slice of quiche in half. "But there are other kinds of strong too."

"Once I heard Daddy call you strong. He said moving back to Toronto and starting over again at forty was strong."

The little ears of an only child.

"Do you ever wish you still lived in Bermuda?"

"No. I love living in the same city as you and your Mummy and Daddy."

Maddy grinned. "Me too. But do you ever miss Uncle Jackson?"

She was surprised that her niece recalled her ex-husband's name. "Do you remember him?"

Madison shrugged. "A little tiny bit, from a long time ago. Mostly I remember the water where you lived. It was pretty." She pointed at Grenadier Pond. "Please will you tell me about the horses now?"

"Well," said Brigitte. "In the winter of eighteen twelve there was a war on and some big soldiers on horseback, called grenadiers, were coming to defend the city. They crossed the pond but the ice had already started to melt and it was thinner than they thought."

Notes towards Recovery

"So there was a big crack and then the ice broke!" Madison took over the story at her favourite part. "It made a big, big hole in the middle of the pond and they couldn't escape. And they all fell through and drowned. Horses and soldiers and all. And no sign of them was ever, ever found again."

Brigitte hugged her niece and smiled. "You know it word for word." She looked out at the blue water, its surface sparkling in the afternoon sunshine.

"But that's not the end. Tell the bit about the mud."

"No one has ever been able to measure how deep the pond is, because the bottom is soft, squishy sediment. So maybe there are lots of things buried down there. Nobody knows what lies beneath."

Madison stared out at the water for a moment then turned her face to look up into Brigitte's eyes. "Maybe if we went scuba diving we could find out for sure? There would be bones and treasures and we could take them to a museum to be put on display in a glass case with a big sign that says do not touch."

"Maybe we could. But right now how about we go and find the llamas and the peacocks? And then the adventure playground?"

Madison wasn't ready to change the subject. "I'm going to learn scuba diving when I'm eight years old, and you're going to teach me, right?"

That was what she'd promised. Before. She said she hoped she wouldn't be too old by then.

"You won't be too old, silly. I'm already six, so that's only two years from now." She held up six fingers then slowly unfurled two more. "Can we have ice cream later?"

"Sure we can. How about a knickerbocker glory?"

"A what?"

"A knickerbocker glory. When I was your age my English grandmother used to take me out for a knickerbocker glory for a special treat. In a café in her favourite store which was pale green and kept honey bees on the roof." She hated moments like this when she couldn't find a name she'd always known. And too late, she remembered that was a London treat, not a Toronto treat. "Anyhow, we'll find some ice cream and you can have any flavour you like."

"A chocolate dipped cone? From Dairy Queen?"

"Sure!"

They had the zoo almost to themselves and there were just a few mothers and nannies with preschool children at the adventure playground. Madison made up a game involving pirates and mermaids and a treasure chest full of gold doubloons and chased her Aunt up and down the ladders, and in and out of the castle turrets until Brigitte had to wave a white flag. "This pirate is pooped," she said, flopping onto a bench and turning her face to catch the last of the afternoon sun on her cheeks. Already she could feel the heat fading and cooler hints of evening in the air. But the long, dark months were over and summer was on its way.

Maddy sat beside her. "I like playing hooky with you. Do you think everyone else in my class is still in school?" She looked down at Brigitte's wrist, rolling the heavy gold chain out of the way to look at her watch, as if she could read time.

"Tell me the story about your bracelet." Another favourite.

"On the day that your Grampa died I was very, very sad. I cried and cried and I didn't know if I'd ever be able to stop, but I knew I had to because it was upsetting your Mummy and Daddy. So I went into the bathroom and washed my face and then I fussed about a bit with makeup to try and hide the red blotches on my cheeks. I found this bracelet in my make-up bag and to give myself just a few more moments to compose myself, I put it on."

Notes towards Recovery

Maddy was running her fingers over the golden rope. "And you've never taken it off, not even once, since that day."

"Never," Brigitte agreed. "Not when I have a manicure, not when I was in Rio at the carnival and someone tried to steal it, not when I went scuba diving." For the MRI she'd had to take it off, but she pushed that thought aside.

Madison kept playing with the bracelet. "And not every time, but often, when you feel it on your wrist, it reminds you of your Daddy."

"That's right." And that was the truth. She rarely connected it to Jackson, even though he had presented it to her with great fanfare after she'd forgiven him for one of his affairs. "But one day I will take it off to give it to you."

"When I'm a bit bigger so it doesn't fall off."

"Yes. I hope that it will remind you of me in the same way. So you don't forget me."

"I'll never forget you. Not even if you moved back to Bermuda. Not even if you never give me your bracelet." Madison snuggled closer, her fingers still entwined in the woven gold chain. "I love you."

"And I love you. But memory is a funny thing, Honey. Sometimes it plays tricks on us and we forget things we thought we could never forget."

"Like Grampa, when he got really old."

She nodded. Could stories of the past be enough of a bond to build a future? She looked down at the bracelet, tempted to give it to her niece right now, and noticed the time. "Yikes. It's already ten past three. We'd better head home." She stood and led the way up the nature trail, pausing when it divided into three paths.

"You promised me ice cream."

So she had. She said they'd stop for ice cream on the way home. There was a Dairy Queen on the corner; they'd walk right by it on their way back. Their way back-

Brigitte turned slowly, trying to get her bearings. The skyline didn't help here, it was all maple, oak, birch, poplar, none in full leaf. Nothing stood out. That way, she thought. But she wasn't sure. "This way," she said, hoping her confusion was masked by the sound of confidence.

They walked for fifteen minutes, though Brigitte tried not to keep looking at her watch. Wasn't this the nature trail in the Spring Creek area, heading north? Or had she gone too far and ended up in the west ravine? She looked up through trees at the sky, trying to figure which way they were walking based on the sun, but she was too flustered to work it out. The ravine, whichever one it was, was starting to feel claustrophobic. The underbrush had the dank smell of rotting leaves and the wind had picked up, cracking twigs. Branches scratched at the sky, then bent down as if to reach for her. Brigitte shivered and picked up her pace, searching for steps up and out of the gorge. A field, relief.

"Why did we come back here?" Maddy's voice had a distinct whine to it.

They'd returned to the zoo. Damn. Except, except that meant she just had to go in the opposite direction from last time, right? She looked at her watch. As soon as they got out of the park and on to a street, any street, she'd hail a taxi and they might still make it home on time.

Brigitte gestured to the ground at their feet. "Did you know that there is an ancient river running underneath our feet that was only just discovered? It's over a million years old and no one knew about it until two thousand and three."

"A million years old? I don't even know how many zeros that is."

Notes towards Recovery

"A lot! And it was just a fluke. Two workers had just put a lid on a well and it blew off like a geyser. It shot water up into the air in a spout as high as your house. So they dug down underneath it and found the river which carries water all the way from Georgian Bay to Lake Ontario."

"I'm cold," said Maddy. As a distraction, the new story hadn't worked.

"Let's run then, and that will warm us up."

"I'm too tired to run." The child sounded on the verge of tears.

"Oh, Honey. I'm sorry. I just took the wrong path." Brigitte knelt down. "Climb up and I'll give you a piggy back."

She'd forgotten how heavy a six year old could be and she had to slow down. Next person we pass, she vowed, I'll ask for directions. But the mothers, nannies and dog walkers had all gone home; it felt as if she and Maddy were all alone in the four hundred acres. They reached the lakeside and she took a deep breath. Okay. If she went south they'd reach the Queensway. So the water should be on her left? No, right hand side. She turned and went the opposite direction.

"We're almost home," she said, hoping she sounded confident.

Four oh four. Four twelve. No sign of any road. They must be going north, instead of south. She couldn't hear any traffic, only her own pounding heart and the ghostly echo of soldiers and horses, skidding on ice, panicked screams as they fell into the freezing water below.

Once before there had been a moment when she'd felt this disorientated. She and Jackson had been diving the Cayman Wall and the clarity had been like nothing she'd ever experienced before. Visibility for hundreds of feet. When she'd looked at her depth gauge she was already at a dangerous one hundred and fifty, but when she started swimming, still looking at her gauge, she found she was still heading down. One sixty. She did a half somersault. One seventy. She somersaulted again but had no way of knowing which direction was which. Only at one eighty did she get herself turned the right way and start going back up.

It had been so peaceful, though. That thick blue silence. That's how I'd choose to commit suicide, she'd decided then, as the silvery underside of the sea's surface had come into view. To drift down through schools of fish and neon corals, pass out and know no more.

"Auntie Brigitte, I'm scared."

"There's nothing to be scared about."

"But you don't know where we are. And I'm going to be late for skating."

"We're on the right path now. We're almost home. I just need to put you down now, though." She should have made this into a game, a continuation of the pirates and mermaids they'd been playing. A hunt for Atlantis. "Can you see the towers of the castle on your street?"

"Not a castle. It's a hospital. And they were smashing it down this morning when Mummy and I walked to school."

The pedestrian walkway past the demolition. Had that only been a few hours ago? She took a breath. "We'll be home soon."

Claire and Philippe were running down their front steps before Brigitte had paid off the taxi. Her brother gathered Madison into his arms and she immediately burst into tears. "We got so lost Daddy and we had to walk forever."

"I'm sorry. I'm sorry," said Brigitte.

"Did I miss skating, Mummy?"

Claire took Madison from Philippe and turned away. "You can go next week, Darling."

Philippe waited until his wife and daughter were in the house before he spoke. 'What the hell Bree? We were worried sick.

Notes towards Recovery

Claire wanted me to phone the police. Couldn't you have called us to tell us you were delayed?"

"Called. She felt inside her handbag. She hadn't once thought of her cell phone, not even when she needed a map. "I'm sorry," she said again. "It started out as a great day. Really. We had a great day. I hope Maddy will remember it as a great day. Her little hand kept reaching for mine and we both felt the first of the summer sun on our faces and-" For the first time since that morning she felt tears.

"You can't dictate what people will remember." He sounded exhausted.

"Philippe. I have to tell you. I saw a neuropsychologist this morning."

Her brother looked at her. "What? What are you talking about?"

"An Alzheimer's specialist."

"Bree-"

"I just needed confirmation of what I've known for a while." Since an evening last winter, when she was late to her own dinner party. She couldn't make it through the recipe she was trying to follow and had to dash out to the grocery store where she'd shopped every week for the previous three years. Getting confused on the way home, she had driven around her neighbourhood for the best part of an hour. That was when she'd known it was real. Not just exhaustion or stress or a heavy workload or a series of bad days.

Today's appointment had given her an official name and a realistic prognosis. "He gave me a bunch of leaflets to read. There's one for siblings who might want to consider being screened for the PS1 mutation. But it's unlikely, very unlikely, he said, since you show no signs of early onset dementia."

"Bree."

94

"I just needed one day with Maddy. Just us. I'm sorry I'm so late and I'm sorry she got cold and tired, I-"

"It's okay. She'll be fine. We'll all be fine." The words fell, grey and flat, in the empty evening.

She wouldn't be allowed to take Maddy out again by herself. Claire wouldn't trust her.

Her brother put his arm over her shoulders. "Come inside. Come and have some supper, a cup of tea. Remember Grandmother and her endless cups of tea?"

"Fortnum and Mason's." That was where they'd had the knickerbocker glories. It wasn't lost forever, that shop's name, but had come back to her, rising as if through feet of thick, sludgy mud, finally reaching the surface. "They kept honeybees on the roof, didn't they? I'm not making that up?"

She remembered too, surfacing from the Cayman Wall dive. Jackson had started yelling before she'd even clambered into the boat. "Fuck, Bridge! What the hell were you doing going so deep? You know about the risk of nitrogen narcosis." He'd pulled her close, wetsuit, tank and all. "I was terrified I'd lose you. I couldn't bear it if I lost you."

Riffle

I'm half an hour late to the morning briefing. What this means is that all the best muffins have been taken from the plate, that the coffee is lukewarm, that a green slip detailing my misdemeanour will be placed in my in-tray this afternoon. The free muffin is the highlight of these jargon-heavy meetings, and I'm stuck with a choice of gluten-free raisin bran or sugar-free cranberry with flaxseeds.

While the manager talks about managing client expectations, specialist challenges, assistive technology, I pick out the raisins, seven of them, and sweep them, along with the crumbs, into a tidy pile by my mug.

"Shirley?"

I have no idea what I've just been asked, what topic we've reached.

"Yes," says my supervisor. She looks at me.

I nod, with no idea with I've agreed to, sit up, pull my shoulders back and try to follow the rest of the discussion. It's Mr. Campbell. He's been 'in God's waiting room' (my supervisor's phrase) since mid-winter but survived the spring and summer and now the leaves are bright red, orange and yellow. I'm on

Notes towards Recovery

night sitting duty with him, a misnomer as my shift starts as soon as the meeting is over.

So it's going to be a good day after all. We aren't supposed to have favourites, but we all do and Mr. Campbell's mine. He arrived in his daughter's car. Against all advice she drove him to the care home, and only asked for my help after it became apparent that, although she had managed to get him into the front seat, she couldn't lift him out by herself.

I had leaned in, smiled at the elderly gentleman, told him I was going to pick him up and that I hoped no one from the health and safety committee was watching. Already that month I'd been sent three of the green warnings. They sat, unread, in my in-tray and occasionally I amused myself by guessing what infractions they cited. Not bending at the knees, not using a hoist as per regulations, not waiting for an aide when a male resident needed bathing, clocking out then continuing to work.

"A pretty young thing like you picking me up," he'd said. I acknowledged the corny line with a chuckle. He was tall, Mr. Campbell, and must have been a commanding presence once, but in old age he'd become as meagre as a newborn calf, shivering, weak, with unsteady legs. It was easy for me to gather him into my arms and lift him into the wheelchair.

His daughter had thanked me, started to say she wasn't as strong as she'd thought and-

I'd brushed away the end of her sentence, said there was a knack to it was all, and taken a step back, allowing her time to fuss with the foot rests and stroke his cheek.

Big boned, my mother still calls me; the town kids used to tease me with nicknames like Burly Shirley. Physically, I am my father's daughter, a Renfrew County farm girl. From my mother I inherited the stubborn gene. You're impossible, impossible, David had said, every time we argued. Sometimes I forget he wasn't the one to leave our marriage; he hadn't stormed out after one of those arguments.

Arguments involving shouting and slammed doors I knew, I understood. The silence between Mr. Campbell's daughter and her brother was foreign to me. That first day her brother had pulled up in a big, expensive car. "All right," he'd said and I hadn't known if he was making a statement or asking a question. If he was talking to me, or his sister, or his father, or himself.

His sister had not answered or made eye contact with him. Instead she'd adjusted the pillow behind the wisps of her father's grey hair one more time. "We don't have to stay, Dad. If you've changed your mind we can turn around and go home right now."

Her brother had said her name. "We've discussed this. We're going to give it a chance."

That would have been two and a half years ago. I've seen him - the brother - perhaps five times since then. The daughter came daily before she moved down south, now she makes the journey once a month. Today is Thanksgiving and they'll both be here.

I'm sitting with Mr. Campbell at a window table, with a view over the river that runs along the bottom edge of the property, where squealing children are daring each other to wade in. When his daughter arrives she stands in the doorway, and I realize she can't see through her tears, so I walk over and offer her a tissue. "Your Dad's having a good day," I tell her. "He's looking forward to your visit." Maybe I've embellished, but surely I should manage families' expectations too. His eyes are open, that's the sign of a good day for him now.

"It's his loss of words... that's the most difficult," she says. "The physical challenges, I think I could bear. But for an editor." When he could still speak he told me stories from his thirty-five years working at the country's largest newspaper. "To have

Notes towards Recovery

to search for basic words or point to a child-like drawing of the simplest items: tea, table, book. It breaks my heart."

He's not been able to point to pictures for weeks. I send a wish out to the universe that Mr. Campbell will say something today, anything, just a few words his daughter can understand.

"Please," she asks me. "Will you stay with us, for lunch?"

I thank her, lead her to the table and pull out the chair next to his wheelchair.

Her brother arrives soon after, nods at us, and sits after awkwardly patting his father's shoulder. He comments on the weather, fine for this time of year, and the delays in town caused by a row of movie trailers, then opens the menu as it's handed to him.

His sister has pulled herself together and takes his lead. "Yes. They've transformed the main street into an American parade route. Red, white and blue bunting, the Stars and Stripes on every flag pole." She continues making cheerful comments about a book she's reading, something about fishing that her Dad would love, and how it sparked a memory of a childhood holiday. In an artificially bright voice she reads the daily specials from the menu's insert: butternut squash soup, maple-braised turkey, pumpkin cheesecake, deep dish apple pie.

When the server comes back, Mr. Campbell's eyes are shut and there's a line of drool from the paralysed side of his mouth. But I translate the shudder of his chin to mean no thank you to a full Thanksgiving dinner. Then he slowly cups his hands together, as if trying to hold water scooped from a stream.

"I know Chef," I say. "He'll cook you anything you like, Mr. Campbell, even if it isn't on the menu. Can you describe what it is?"

Silence, then the hint of a whisper. I lean closer. "I missed that, sorry. Can you tell me again, please?"

"Fragile."

Fragile. I try to think of delicate foods. Mille-feuille, with its layers of puff pastry? Meringues? Spun sugar? He doesn't react to any of my suggestions then cups his hands together again.

I cup my own hands together. Fragile, I think. And of my own broken body and of my pilgrimage this morning, the reason I was late. "Eggs. Eggs?"

And he manages a nod.

"Well that's easy." I smile. "And how can I have Chef fix them for you? An omelet, Eggs Benedict, poached on spinach with cheese sauce?"

His tilted chin indicates no but this time I'm sure one side of his mouth looks content.

"Fried, over easy, sunny side up? Soft boiled with soldiers? Coddled? Kedgeree? Huevos rancheros?" I fill the silence with a grin. "I grew up on a farm with chickens and ate eggs every day of my childhood. I can keep going."

"Mixed up," he says. His whisper is clear and I beam at his daughter.

'Mixed up. Scrambled! Scrambled eggs."

"Scrambled. Yes. Like my words."

Not only clear speech, full sentences, but a joke. I laugh, and his daughter leans over to hold his hands. "Dad!" Her voice is light and her brother looks up from the cell phone he's been studying, tapping at.

Live in the present, the therapist tried to teach me. Let go of the past and the future and engage in the moment. I'd like to tell Mr. Campbell's daughter to hold this moment. Hold fast to this moment.

I do know Chef, this much is true. I may have exaggerated his pleasure at cooking a la carte on one of his busiest days, but I stand at his turkey and stuffing covered pass making it clear

Notes towards Recovery

I have no intention of leaving until he's made me three plates of creamy, fluffy eggs. He shouts a bit and throws the pan into the sink when he's finished, but I notice he's added triangles of buttered toast with the crusts cut off and garnished the plates with a rosette of smoked salmon, grilled cherry tomatoes, finely chopped parsley.

I deliver the lunch and sit, feeding Mr. Campbell tiny mouthfuls with the spoon from his coffee cup, catching the dribbles with a soft paper napkin.

The brother eats quickly, then returns his attention to the phone next to his plate, as if whoever he's texting is more worthy of his time than his father. And who am I to assume - I've seen people deal with grief in myriad ways. Or maybe he needs to nail a contract in order to pay the care home's bill. When his sister struggles to find small talk enough for a one-sided conversation I contribute, guessing at the movie being filmed in town, suggesting we watch the fake parade the next day. "Shall we go along for a laugh, Mr. Campbell? We could be extras in the film. Some big shot Hollywood producer might spot you and offer you a contract." I feed him another bite of eggs.

He chews slowly and swallows with difficulty, his eyes opening and closing. After a few more bites he reaches his right hand for his chest.

"That's our code for enough, or thank you," I explain to his daughter. My heart is full.

She tries to smile. "You look tired, Dad,' she says. 'Let's get you settled down for an afternoon siesta and I'll read to you for a bit. ' She stands. No eye contact with her brother.

I wheel Mr. Campbell to his room, hoist and settle him into bed, then say goodbye and turn to leave them, but his son follows me out into to the hall. "I admire your patience," he says. "That meal would have been . . difficult . . without you."

As close to 'thank you', I suspect, as he's able to manage. "It's easier for me," I say. "I'm not family, don't have that emotional connection." I don't add that I have the time. No children, no husband anymore, and my own parents both fit and well.

We hear her voice through the open door. "Okay Dad? Comfy?" Waiting, as though to catch an answer.

"She won't know what to do," he says. "Without him she'll be lost."

"Your parents raised an able woman," I say. "And she's got you."

He shakes his head. "I don't remember the childhood details, which story goes with which memory, all that stuff that's so important to her." Now we hear her tears. "Dad. I love you. I love you."

Be there for her, I want to tell him. But I don't. He must be able to hear that she's saying goodbye, he must know they're both saying goodbye. I leave before my own tears give me away. I'm not irreplaceable and one day I'll lose this job as a result of my refusal to follow the rules I consider unnecessary. But maybe I'll surprise everyone, David most of all, and hand in my notice before I'm fired.

An hour later she finds me at the front desk. "You're my Dad's favourite," she says. "He told me he'd like you to have this." She's holding out a metal prong. "He ran the slot in the old days," she explains. "Before computers, he cut stories with a pair of pinking sheers and this was for the ones that got spiked."

When I come out from behind the desk and take the spike, heavier than I expected, she clutches at me, whispers urgently. "Please. No heroic measures."

"No heroic measures." I put down the spike, meet her gaze and make it clear I understand what she's saying.

Notes towards Recovery

"I think he's- I know I'm not making it easy for him. I have to let him go. I wish- I-"

I know. I know. I comfort her as I imagine a mother would comfort a child, with gentle sounds and the offer of a hug. We're not allowed physical contact with patients' guests but I pretend I've forgotten that, as I often do. As she starts to sob on my shoulder I pat her back, murmur, reach in my pocket for a tissue.

"Will you and your brother spend this afternoon together, so you won't be alone?" I ask.

"We drove up separately." She blows her nose. "He's a good man. I know he can appear… . But he's a good man. He used to read the newspaper out loud, when Dad's eyesight first started going, all the articles he knew Dad would enjoy."

"I'll read to your father this afternoon," I promise. "Sit with him as long as he likes." And when she leaves I walk back to his room, where Mr. Campbell is lying exactly as I left him, facing the window that looks towards the river.

"Thank you so much," I say, hefting the spike like a trophy. I'm not allowed to accept a gift from a patient, and certainly such a dangerous thing as this must be against the rules. "I love it. I'm going to impale all my health and safety warnings on it. I'm going to set it in the middle of my desk and just let those green forms pile up into Christmas tree."

I put it down on the bedside table beside a military history book, and sit in the still-warm easy chair beside his bed. "Shall I read?" I pick up the book.

His breathing is more laboured than it was at lunch. I meet his gaze and he blinks twice. No.

"What would you like to hear?" I ask.

I have time to wait for the answer. After some time it comes. "Your words."

My words. I close the book and put it down.

"I drove past my old house this morning," I tell him. "The sugar maple we planted, my husband and I, is beautiful. Deep reds, bright oranges."

His eyes flicker.

And I talk. I tell him what I've never told anyone else. That buried under that tree is a series of letters I wrote to my stillborn baby, the one I'd been promised I'd carry full term. I never heard her heartbeat, not even once, I say. I tell him that those secret letters were the real reason I'd fought against moving, even though it was necessary for my husband's job. That I had waited until today, Thanksgiving, to drive past it, just the once. That once had been enough; now I could let go. Say goodbye.

His eyes are closed and his breathing is inaudible. But he reaches his good hand for mine, and, holding my wrist, slowly pulls my hand over his chest.

"Thank you," I say. "Mine too. My heart is full." I put my other hand on top of his and feel his chest rise and fall, weak, weaker. We sit like this, a haze of wood smoke from a nearby bonfire drifting into the silence around us.

A sunbeam crosses the room and I think he notices. I look outside. "There's a riffle in the river just below your window," I tell him. "Sometimes this time of year we see the salmon running." I ask him if he ever fished this river. It's catch-and-release, and some weekends I see fishermen in the shallows. I imagine out loud what power it is that allows a salmon to navigate its way back to its natal spawning ground to lay eggs before death.

As I say that word, death, my voice catches and I look out the window again, imagining a salmon leaping, twisting, its scales catching the light.

"The beauty of the trees," I quote. "The softness of the air."

And there is a sudden softness under my hand. A quivering, and then a suggestion of space.

Notes towards Recovery

I finish reciting Chief Dan George's poem. "The strength of the fire, the taste of the salmon, the trail of the sun, and the life that never goes away, they speak to me. And my heart soars."
Later, after I've spoken with my supervisor, and called Mr. Campbell's children, I am going to call David. My heart is full with you and I, I'll say. Please forgive me, I'll ask.
I try it now.
"Please forgive me."
It is a good and gentle sound.

Granny Squares

This weekend's plan has been fixed for some time and I am pleased today has arrived. After a year and a half of pretending that my mother in law was able to live by herself, it is a relief to arrive at her house armed with boxes, rubber gloves and cleaning supplies. This, I can do. Cleaning out the fridge, scrubbing the oven I've been unplugging after every visit, retrieving the hidden kettle, knives, matches, things that could have been dangerous if left unattended. Washing down walls, sweeping, dusting, minor repairs. It's not a weekend I've been looking forward to, but by tomorrow evening I'll feel a sense of satisfaction at a job well done. The house will be clean, bare, odourless - I can imagine it already.

"We can't throw anything out," Laurent has warned me, many times, even though he himself, if he had no siblings, would pay a firm to come in and empty the house so he could get it on the market and sold. We both know agreeing to terms for the sale will take another eighteen months, but it's this sale which will pay the bill for the care home, with its suite of rooms big enough for three shelves of books Mémère will never again read.

By 'we' he means 'you' - he means me. A few weeks after I had weaned our second son and was able to enjoy a drink again,

Notes towards Recovery

we celebrated with an impromptu party that involved our best friends, cocktails, bowls of pasta, and more bottles of red wine than planned. I hadn't seen him so endearingly drunk since our courting days and despite a moment of panic (I must be a bad mother; what if one of us needs to drive the toddler or the baby to the hospital in the middle of the night?) it was a good evening. When our friends finally tumbled into taxis or stumbled off down the street Laurent turned to me and gestured around the living room. "Darling Jessie." *Jezzie*. "I'm too drunk to list you all the reasons I love." I responded to this sweet garbled message by taking him to the kitchen, filling a pint glass with water, and passing it to him. Drink this now, I suggested, for a better morning. But he was determined to finish his speech. "No clutter," he said. "You keep no clutter. I adore that, you, and I don't know if I've ever said."

He hadn't, but now, when I'm culling the coffee table of magazines and he sneaks an unfinished one from the pile, or I'm boxing up a forgotten yet suddenly favourite item for Goodwill and he protests, I tease him. No clutter. You adore me because we live in a house with no clutter.

My mother-in-law wasn't a hoarder, but she kept herself busy by making things. She tatted doilies for armrests and knitted teapot covers and decorated lacy containers for boxes of tissues, and plastic stick dolls with frou-frou skirts to hide extra rolls of toilet paper. Does anyone make that sort of doll anymore, or is it lost, that 1970s craft? Laurent's childhood home was very different from mine and I loved visiting; it was like a trip to a foreign place. Only after my father-in-law was put into care did I fully appreciate how much he had done to contain his wife's chaos. Over the next five years, side tables, window sills and finally the kitchen countertops disappeared under piles of stuff. Junk. Amassed and accumulated and unearthed from the attic when she could still pull down the ladder in the hallway and get up there to root around.

"We can't throw anything out," my husband says again as they arrive. "Not before Claudine gets here."

"Understood." And I do understand. My sister-in-law, only barely recovered from her father's long slide into dementia and death, fought the move of her mother into a home until, finally, Mémère got the curtains caught in the toaster oven, left on while she sat down to 'read' in an easy chair and, of course, fell asleep. If the window hadn't been open a crack, if the wind hadn't blown the smoke in the neighbour's direction... No suggestion it was anything other than old age and memory loss, but social services were called and Claudine, as eldest, was offered choices. Move someone in full time, or move Mémère out.

I give the boys the energetic outside chores: raking the leaves then mowing the lawn. Getting up on a ladder to clear maple shoots and moss from the gutters. Sweeping the paths and driveway. Tackling the garden. We've bribed them with promises of a double junk food day - pizza for lunch and Chinese for supper. But Gabriel and Mathis would have come without the incentive. They understand the importance to me of helping family. Pépère lived in the care home, a different one than his wife has been moved in to, for over five years. All those Sundays of their childhood we got the boys up early, drove here to collect Mémère, and took them both to Mass then out to lunch. Even when Pépère had no idea who we were, was no longer able to string words together, French or English, that made any sense, we got up every Sunday and repeated the process. More than one dark winter morning Laurent groaned as the alarm went off and suggested we skip it, no one would notice. I'd notice, I said. It wasn't for his parents by then, it was for me; I was safeguarding my own old age, setting this example and counting on my sons to

Notes towards Recovery

bring their wives, their children, to visit me should I grow feeble and deranged.

Claudine arrives three hours later than the agreed time then sits in the car for about ten minutes after she's parked. "Watch out Tante Claudine," the boys yell from the roof as they sweep leaves to the driveway, and that seems to break her trance. She gets out, waves at the boys and then sighs - I see her whole torso rise and fall, imagine I can hear her through the window - and comes inside.

I thought about bringing decent coffee and a perk, but didn't want to add to the pile we'd have to take home, so have instead a jar of fancy instant coffee, the leftovers of which needn't be kept. I've boiled the kettle, and put cookies on a plate (my white chocolate and raspberry ones she once claimed to like - I had thought about making one of Mémère's recipes but that seemed too risky).

I greet my sister-in-law at the door with a hug and say nothing about the time, or her red eyes, then call Laurent up from the basement, suggesting we all sit and relax for a moment. "Laurent is starting with the workshop and the boys are doing some outside work," I tell Claudine. "I've cleaned the bathrooms and kitchen."

"What have you done with all the food? The jams and all the tins?" There is a note of panic in her voice, she doesn't even say hello to her brother.

Kept them all, I reassure her, then ask if maybe she knows of a food bank. Though I'm aware a food bank would have to throw them all away, not a single tin is even within a year of its best-before date and there's a date loaf that is older than both my children. She nods, agreeing, and Laurent gently kicks me under the table. We both know they won't be dropped off a food bank, that Claudine will give them space in her basement cold room and never eat them, perhaps occasionally holding one of them as some sort of talisman. A picture of her with the ancient date loaf is so vivid that I blink back a tear and maybe that's what allows her to relax her shoulders, though she still doesn't sit, or touch the mug of coffee.

"I wrote a list," she says, patting her pockets but not reaching inside any of them. "I don't know what I've done with it." She inspects the kitchen, running her hand across the cracked laminate counter as if it's Italian marble, then stands at the window untying and re-tying the faded gingham curtains.

"We thought it would be best if you pack up your mum's room," I say. "I'll box up the books downstairs." The basement is lined with built-in shelving, half of it filled with books, the rest a mess of junk which should all go into garbage bags and recycle bins, but I know Claudine will need to examine each item before deciding its fate. A job for the evening perhaps, helped along with several glasses of wine.

Her back stiffens. "Not the books. You can't do the books. I need to sort them first."

"We don't have enough time for that," says Laurent.

"What do you mean?" says Claudine, turning towards her brother. "We can take as long as we need."

Laurent shakes his head. "We agreed. One weekend, get it done."

"No." His sister shakes her head. "If I need longer… I will need longer. I never agreed."

My husband says nothing.

I want to reach out and touch her arm, remind her that when the tip of his nose goes white like this it's a sign to back off. "It'll be fine," my voice sounds artificial even to my own ears. "We'll get it all done. And Yvette said she might come by tomorrow to help if she's having a good day." All those years of church-going

Notes towards Recovery

did not make me a better person - I am aware that a poorly day for the eldest sister will make our lives easier.

"I'm going to sort the books," Claudine says, moving towards the stairs.

Laurent stands. "No." It is his cold voice, the one he rarely uses. Enough, it says. No more discussion. "You were meant to be here at eight. It's after eleven. You've forfeited the choice to do the books. Lisa will pack them up and you can sort them out at home."

"That means I'll get first pick. You'll miss out on any you want." Clearly a threat.

"We don't want any of these books," says Laurent. "You can take them all or we can go and dump them at Goodwill right now."

Deliver, I think. *Deliver* would have been a better verb choice than dump. But it's too late. The conversation escalates to an argument, about- About Laurent putting his foot down, insisting that Mémère's house be emptied of all her possessions and sold. Though that's never said, I hear it in every terse sentence. Claudine stumbles over an idiom and reverts to Québécois for a tirade, and I am thankful that Laurent says nothing in reply. She ends by spitting something I don't understand, clumping upstairs and slamming a hallway door behind her with such force the whole house shakes.

Laurent looks at me. "I'm sorry," he says. "I didn't-" He sighs. "I thought I could make it through the first morning at least."

"Everyone's stressed," I say, rubbing his shoulders, willing him to relax. I was worried I'd be the one to lose my temper, it never occurred to me that my good-natured, even-keeled husband would blow. "And we've got lots of time, two full days - we'll get this done." If I have to pull an all-nighter I will.

We kiss, reaffirming the lack of animosity between us. Then he takes three cookies and goes back down to the workshop. I pour the cold coffee down the sink and stand at the window looking at the view which is framed by the yellow and white gingham. This is what my mother-in-law looked at for fifty-eight years. A sloping lawn, a steep tree-covered hill, and then the river. Over the time she lived here those trees, a mixture of birch and poplar, must have grown into the forest they are now. And the river, of course, is different every moment. I imagine her standing here on the day they moved in, amazed at her luck, and as the seasons turned, grateful for all her blessings.

Her view now, through a discreetly barred window, is a window box the boys gave her, beyond that a busy road and a strip mall. I blink and turn away, surprised at my sentimentality. Basement. Boxes. Books. But first I make a fresh cup of coffee and take it upstairs. Claudine is pulling everything from the closet, dumping it in a pile on her mother's bed. I put the coffee and two cookies down on the lace-topped bedside table and reach to pat her back in what I hope will be perceived as a gesture of support.

"Don't be nice to me or I'll start to cry," she says in French. "I don't know how you put up with my brother, that stubborn mule. You must be a saint. Or an idiot." She turns away and keeps pulling clothes from the closet as I leave the room.

She was always going to take it the hardest of the siblings - well, the three siblings I know. I wonder what Annick, if asked, would say about her mother, the house and all its possessions. I take care with the books, as if that might somehow help to ease Claudine's pain. I blow off the dust, and semi-sort the books that will sit in these boxes in her house for months, perhaps longer. Books should be read. There are charity stores in the city that would put them out on shelves, sell them for almost nothing, so

Notes towards Recovery

they could be taken home by strangers who would open them, perhaps enjoy them.

As if to compensate for their years of neglect, I say their titles out loud. An eclectic mix, in no order at all. *Birds of Northeastern Quebec*. A Pierre Berton novel. Essays. A glossy photo book of Maritime lighthouses. *Narrowboaters' Guide to Yorkshire's Churches*. I can't remember a story of my parents-in-law visiting Yorkshire, much less by narrowboat, and I make a mental note to ask over lunch - surely this is a safe topic.

I'd allotted twelve boxes and an hour to this chore, but hadn't planned to sort as I packed. Now I do. Non-fiction, fiction, hardbacks, one box for French language, another for sun-bleached, dog-eared novels which I label 'cottage.' The shelves are three-books deep, and I start to feel like an archeologist going back through layers of history. *Valley of the Dolls*. Mad magazine anthologies. Children's picture books. I label a new box: Children/ YA, and wonder if they should go to the cottage as well. How long before we are the oldest generation?

I need a chair to reach the piles on the higher shelves, sneeze several times as I bring them down and years' worth of dust clouds the air. These ones need a damp washcloth and still there is a layer of sticky grime. But I've realized I can do all the basement shelves; I box all the knickknacks for Claudine to take home and sort at her leisure, when she's ready. Until there's only the very top shelf left. I glance at my watch. Time before lunch to finish and wash down the shelves.

The last book down is a photo album, maroon cover with illegible gold writing on the front. *Our Family* perhaps? I look at a few pages of faded snapshots with rounded corners. Picnics and birthday parties and a canoe trip. Good. Another safe lunchtime activity - it must have been years since either Laurent or Claudine has seen any of these pictures.

As I let hot water fill a bucket in the laundry room, I text Gabe, asking him to please order pizza for delivery. Ask your Tante what she'd like.

A reply comes instantly. If we could drive it'd be faster and cheaper.

Yes, I say, but illegal, adding a smiley emoticon. There are probably push bikes in the garage you can use. May need to pump up the tires. I add bright yellow cleanser to the bucket, breathing in the smell of fake lemon that says to me, clean. I'm surprised at the message that comes back: yeah okay we'll bike. Take my wallet, I text, in my handbag in the entryway. The sound of footsteps clattering up the stairs and moments later the sound of the front door. This time next year Gabe will be driving, and applying to universities, and two years later Matt. I'm not ready to be an empty-nester and I attack the bookshelves with excessive force.

It takes three buckets to get the worst of the dirt from the shelves and I wonder if the new owners will fill the space with their own books or tear them down in order to install a big screen TV. When I've emptied the last bucket of dark grey water, I go to the workshop, so barren I barely recognize the room. Laurent looks up from behind a wall of boxes, most of which he's marked with an X in blue Sharpie, and holds a single finger across his lips, then winks. Eighteen years of marriage - we understand each other's codes. All of this then, is not going to his own workshop but to The Mall - a covered section of our local dump where people recycle useable but unwanted items.

I leave the photo album on the kitchen counter and go up to Claudine. She's finished emptying her mother's closet onto the bed and is sitting on the floor; it's difficult to tell what else, if anything she's done since I left. "What can I do to help? Shall I fold some of these?"

Notes towards Recovery

When she doesn't reply I look down at her, but it still takes me a moment to realize that tears are coursing down her face. I sit next to her and pass her a tissue.

"Look," she says, opening a shoe box on her lap. "Look." The box is full of crocheted hexagons in dull colours, each about the size of a child's palm. I recoil at the smell: must and mildew and every cigarette ever smoked in this house for more than four decades.

But I have to say something. "Goodness. What are they?"

"Granny squares. Eight boxes full," says Claudine. "She made them the year I was thirteen."

Forty-five years ago. "Goodness." I'm not sure what else I can say. "That's a lot of crocheting. What could they be used for, I wonder?"

"Anything. Coasters, if you back them. Or you can join them up for afghans or handbags... Mémère had a coat. For that in between fall-winter season, all reds and russets with big patch pockets."

I fix a smile on my face, make myself hold up a few of the wool hexagons as if admiring them. Do not, my inside voice is screaming, do not make me something from these things. Not a coat. Not even a single coaster. I will not give these space in my house. I will not. I unclench my teeth, reminding myself that I don't get to make all the choices. If Laurent has fond memories of these things, then of course we'll house some. A few.

I stand up, and help Claudine stand as well. The boys will be back with lunch soon, I say, and as if on cue, I hear the front door open. From the top of the stairs I watch Gabriel and Mathis walking towards the kitchen with a tower of boxes and two bags, and I point at them, smiling. "Looks like they've bought enough for a dozen people."

Chicken wings, it turns out, and cheese sticks to compliment the cheese-stuffed crust super supreme, and a dessert pizza too, sickly sweet cookie dough covered in mini marshmallows, tiny candies and stripes of chocolate sauce. Seemingly oblivious to any stress between their father and their Tante, they chat about their plans for the winter, a new video game they know we won't buy them but figure they should mention, what with Christmas coming and all, how much faster it would have been to drive to the pizza place than cycle. When they've scarfed down as much as they want ("for now," Matt clarifies) they ask what job they should do next.

I want to grin at Laurent: look how well we've done raising these good, kind kids, but I know enough to say nothing that could be misconstrued as bragging, or worse, a dig at Claudine's children, one of whom moved out west and sends only occasional cards, the other of whom was not only fired from her firm but stripped of her accountancy qualifications after a series of fraudulent practices came to light. Last we heard she was working 'in catering' in Ottawa, which Laurent translated as making coffee at Tim's or perhaps serving ribs and beer to students.

I send our boys off to haul the boxes from the basement. Workshop boxes into the back of the van, books and knickknacks into Claudine's car.

"Surely you don't want all that junk from the basement shelves," Laurent says to his sister. If I could reach his ankle under the table from where I'm sitting, I'd kick him. I know he's trying to be helpful, and his tone is playful, but can't he see how vulnerable a state she's in?

"It was always junk to you," she says. "But some of these things are my childhood treasures."

"Speaking of treasures," I say, passing them each a mug of the instant coffee. "Let's move to the couch. I bet you guys haven't

Notes towards Recovery

seen these in a while." I position myself between them with the photo album on my lap, and open it to the first page.

Laurent wipes some grime from the plastic covering and peers at a snapshot of Mémère and Pépère sitting in a hanging chair on a narrow white porch, two children squished between them. "If ever," he says, wonder in his voice.

Apart from a single formal wedding portrait which lived on the mantelpiece for as long as I can remember, I don't think I've ever seen photos of my in-laws where they look so young. "Is that your house in Val-d'Or?"

"Not *his* house," says Claudine. "*He* never lived there." Fierce resentment in her voice.

Laurent laughs. "Yes, don't forget I'm only a Franco-Ontarian, not a real Québécois." He rolls his eyes.

Claudine continues as if he hadn't spoken. "No outhouse for the miracle child. No sharing a single bedroom with two other children. No three-mile walk to school." She's stiff beside me.

So this is not going to broker peace in the way I'd hoped. I shut the album. "Maybe not such a good time, eh."

But Laurent opens it again, turns the page to a series of photos of a chubby baby on a snowbank, crawling away from the photographer in every frame but one.

"I've never seen these. Who is that, do you think?"

"Yvette," Claudine says. Her body has softened beside me. "That was a pale pink snowsuit, new for her from the Eaton's catalogue. There was a kitten appliquéd on the front."

"We should take these in to show your mother," I say. "Don't you think she'd love to see them?"

Laurent nods, turns the page. The same baby in the same snowsuit, sharing Mémère's lap with a toddler. And a close up of the toddler with marshmallow all over her face. "And that must be Annick," says Laurent. He looks around me to his sister.

"Marshmallows in winter is a fun idea," I say. My voice has once again taken on that irritating false note of cheer.

"I don't remember a single winter campfire," says Laurent.

Claudine turns on him "Well tant pis for toi!" and I start at the malice in her voice.

Laurent is also clearly surprised. "I'm not complaining, I just… You had an extra thirteen years with her. I'm jealous of the things you did before I was born. The energy she had then."

Claudine was silent, and I wondered if perhaps she had never thought of it that way. But her next words are arctic. "You had no idea. You knew nothing. She wasn't well until the year you were born."

I am confused. Mémère's only been unwell for the past few years.

But this is not my mother, not my discussion. I try to stand, thinking I'll slip away and help the boys lug boxes, clean out the garage, anything, but Claudine pushes down on my thigh in order to glare at her brother, effectively trapping me to the sofa.

"You did not know my mother," she says now.

"*Our* mother. I know her," says Laurent. "I love her-"

"You never loved her as much as I do," his sister whispers. "I love her more than my own self." She grabs the album from me and turns the page with force, jabbing her finger at photographs that I barely have a chance to see. "Sailing. None of us could swim. Canoeing in the spring run-off. No lifejackets. Feeding a bear. By hand. Another bonfire," it's almost the height of the house. "After six weeks of drought." As she carries on, her voice rising, the snapshots take on a forbidding look. Now I can see how not-quite-right they are, more like a stage set, hastily constructed and unsafe.

"She wanted an idyllic childhood for us - the picnics, the day trips. She used to yell at me to take a photograph, so you will

Notes towards Recovery

remember this moment, remember it always." She turns a few more pages and all the photographs pass by in a blur. Yvette and Annick age before my eyes, but Claudine is never in the frame. Then a single photograph falls on to the floor. Laurent picks it up, turns it over. "Wait. I remember this castle."

I look at the grainy snapshot with its rounded edges. Mémère is standing at the entrance gates of a red brick building, a mishmash of Victorian and Gothic, arched windows and round towers. To her side, three girls and in her arms, a toddler dressed in a blue wool suit.

Laurent brushes off the dust. "That is me. That must be me. I remember that suit, it was so scratchy. And I- I'm sure I remember chocolate." He keeps staring at the photo in his hand as if looking for answers.

"Yes. The nurses loved you. A happy baby boy. We were all given Easter eggs but yours was the biggest. And many of the residents gave you treats as well." Decades later, hurt at the unfairness still in her voice.

"Nurses," Laurent says.

"City Psychiatric. Toronto. Or as it was called then, the hospital for Psychiatric Maladies and Nervous Disorders."

There is a long silence.

No wonder Claudine had fought so hard against having her mother committed to a care home. I think of Yvette and her 'bad days' and of Annick, the sister-in-law I've never met, and of our sons. Our young, strong, healthy sons. "What- what illness was it?"

Claudine shakes her head. "The name?" She shrugs. "She was given many names. And many drugs. And finally electric shock therapy, which worked."

It is Laurent who is now stiff beside me. "I didn't know," he says, several times. "I'm sorry, I didn't know. I thought we shared a childhood. I had no idea."

"No." Her body softens a little. "How could you?" She takes the photo from his hand, puts it back in the book. "That was her last outpatient treatment. Then she was declared fully recovered."

I am still struggling to reconcile the gentle old woman I know with this mother who seems to put her children in danger. Over and over again. Claudine turns to the last page of the album. The same building, a similar pose. Three girls only, no son, and the girls much younger. This must have been the day she was first released from the hospital. Mémère is wearing a long coat, autumnal colours, reds, russets, big patch pockets. There must be a hundred of the crocheted granny squares stitched together.

"And nine months after she came home," Claudine says, her voice a whisper. "The son she'd always wanted."

"She did get better," Laurent says. He reaches across my lap to hold his sister's hand. "A full recovery."

He will tell me some days later, after we have made love; he will tell me that his mother's full recovery had been beneficial to her and to his father, and to him. But his sisters, he thinks, by the time their mother was well, were already too broken.

Claudine keeps staring at the photograph of the women in the long coat. "That's when she made them all," she says. "In the hospital." A long pause. "I want them to remind me of Mémère's recovery and homecoming. Not of her illness."

"I've always wanted to learn how to crochet," I lie. "Maybe - Maybe you could teach me? Maybe we could crochet together?"

Fiddleback Symphony

I SONATA

I find my sister in the nursing home's common room. Wince at the deep purple bruise under her chin.

"Aleatory. Rubato," she says. Then she strings together more words which, to a foreigner, might sound like sentences. The words are English, her eyes meet mine as she speaks. Her voice rises as if asking a question, pauses for commas and full stops. But random words, in random order.

She's sitting in an easy chair by the picture window that faces the front drive and its row of sugar maples, all reds and yellows, and it is easy for me to pretend she has been watching out for me. I know she doesn't recognize me. But she's happy to see what it is I carry. And suddenly, sense. "My fiddle. Good."

"Hello Norma." I lean in to kiss her cheek, but she pulls back, turns her head away, while at the same time reaching for the violin case. The sight of the angry-looking bruise makes me hesitate and I understand why one of the nurses once hinted at elder abuse.

It doesn't seem to bother her; she lifts the violin and places it against the contusion, closes her eyes and slowly, carefully, draws the bow across the strings to warm up with a series of scales and etudes.

Notes towards Recovery

It was our mother who taught Norma to play the violin, starting with folk songs that she herself had grown up with over on the island. When she realized how especially talented her daughter was, she saved up, first for sheet music, then for lessons from a retired music teacher down the highway.

I sang in the school choir, along with all the other kids, and at church every Sunday, but I didn't get the musical gene. I was never jealous, because of the sixteen years between us or because even I understood that music was the only special treat Norma got.

I was the miracle child, Mother told me when I was young and cuddled in her lap. I'd take down the black and white family portrait that hung in the front hall and name my siblings one by one. My brother, Walter, who had moved out West looking for work, found a widow woman with three children and a wheat farm and stayed. (I didn't meet him until I was twelve, and then it was hard to match the stoop-shouldered man with the freckled teenager in the picture.) Then Marlene and Beverly, both killed by an influenza epidemic the winter after the photograph had been taken, Norma, and finally Evelyn who was lost to consumption the spring before I was born. "I'm not there," I used to tease. "Dorothy isn't there."

"Look for the twinkle in your mother's eye," she would answer, reminding me that my name meant 'gift from God. ' A miracle child, a gift from God. It's remarkable that my head didn't swell up so big I couldn't get through the narrow doorway into the parlour where, after the last of the day's chores was finished, we'd gather, us and any of the kin or farmhands currently there, and Norma would tune up her fiddle and play for us all.

Just as she's doing now. And all the old people stop talking because they know what's coming. My sister, Norma.

II ANDANTE

She starts with a hymn, quoting from the Revelation as she plays the first notes. This is why I drive across Halifax to visit her and this is why that bruise is never given the time it needs to heal. The music she plays and lyrics she hums cut through the dementia. Her hands move, her toes tap time and she comes back, her features softening into someone I recognize.

Dear Refuge of my Weary Soul. This hymn was a favourite of our mother's; I recall her humming it as she baked bread, fed chickens, beat dust from the carpets hanging on the clothes line. She was a believer in refuge, and it was her taking in borders that got our family through the Depression, though there were several she never charged. One winter she gave the neighbours the last of our kerosene so we had none for our lamps; we huddled round the wood stove in the dark and in my imagination Mother sang this very song.

Love Divine All Loves Excelling. Norma is now fully in focus.

It was accepted as fact that mother had married beneath herself. She was a schoolteacher and daughter of a doctor, my father only a farm hand. But they were in love and they were lucky. A second cousin on the mainland needed help and took them in, Mother as the housekeeper and Pa to work the land and when the cousin passed on they inherited it all. And that house was the house where I was born, where Norma lived 'til three years ago.

"Your sister's having episodes," the district nurse told me, calling me from the local hospital. "She's been found lost." Well which one? In my panic I might have snapped.

Notes towards Recovery

"An off-moment," Norma had corrected the diagnosis when I went to see her. An off-moment: the term mother had used when she dropped a vase, missed a step, was unable to stop her hand from shaking. An off-moment. I translated Norma's words and I worried.

She should have married, had a passel of children and a farm of her own, but when I asked her once why she never had, she shook her head and said I'd be more fortunate. (As it turns out, I wasn't.) There was money put aside to send her to college. The summer she left the local schoolhouse an extra hog was slaughtered and sold to cover the costs.

But Norma stayed. She became a seamstress, making as well, all my clothes. I tell her often about the shoddy workmanship of my store-boughten outfits and remember how she matched stripes, hemmed by hand, smocked at the neckline. Those clothes fit me perfectly. A tall child, I had to stand in the back row for the class photograph but I wish I'd been one of the girls in the front so I could remember those dresses more clearly.

There was more money by the time I was ready for college and I went, leaving Norma to care for the last of the farm and our mother. She made wedding dresses for young girls until handmade went out of vogue and then she sewed curtains and soft furnishings, played the organ in church on Sundays, and her violin, always.

After her 'off-moment' I tried taking her back to the house where she knew her way around the rooms, the yard, the gardens. But I had to start playing tricks on her, unplugging the stove when I went out, hiding the matches. When she could no longer bathe or clothe herself if I wasn't there, and I worried that she wasn't eating, I found her this nursing home, known for its work with music and dementia care. And an emphasis, the manager assured me, on non-verbal forms of communication. As if he knew that soon after she arrived my sister would stop speaking any sort of English that I would be able to understand.

III SCHERZO

The hymns over, a sly look comes over her face. Johnny be Fair. Shove it Home. The Moose. Uncle Chet's bawdy songs from his logging camp days. I pretend to look embarrassed for the sake of the staff.

He wasn't our uncle and his name wasn't Chet but one year he arrived with the farmhands who came east from northern Quebec every threshing season. Mother welcomed him as she welcomed them all. Made them strip down and bathe out in the front yard. She scrubbed them herself, and cut their hair and trimmed their beards. She burned the clothes they'd arrived in and gave them a new set to wear, and told them to stay outside for a couple of days until she was sure all the lice had been killed. Then, when she was satisfied that the men were clean she had them fashion long tables in the yard, plywood on sawhorses, and she covered them with food. Fried chicken, baked ham, meatloaf. Stuffed eggs, potato salad and slaw. Tomatoes, pickles and four or five desserts. Though we were Baptist and didn't drink, the same rules didn't hold for the help and jugs of lemonade sat next to mason jars of moonshine.

Sometime after dusk the men with mouth organs and fiddles and banjos would get them out, someone would upturn Ma's tub to make a washtub bass and everyone else would sing and clap. Norma would be called upon to play first, some of the local folk tunes, but as the night wore on and the 'shine passed from hand to hand, the songs grew more and more raunchy. What does that mean, I'd ask when everyone laughed. Why is that funny? By the

127

Notes towards Recovery

time I was old enough to understand the words I knew them all by heart.

The Sleeping Scotsman. Many of the other residents know a version of the song and join in, but in place of the nursing home's harsh electric light, I see the glow of the fire bouncing off the jars, smell the harsh lye soap mother insisted on using, taste that one last mouthful of apple cobbler I ate even as I was falling asleep in Uncle Chet's lap.

Some of the men came and went, but Chet came back every year. He was my favourite, and his arrival a fixture in my calendar. He liked it jes fine, he'd say, when younger, more modern men complained about mother's bossiness, her burning the clothes and setting strict rules. He never complained when the other men teased him. He was my favourite and he spoiled me rotten, carving me dollhouse furniture, carrying me on his shoulders and telling me stories in all the voices. He sang every song, making up words if he didn't know them, and my mother never once hushed him.

IV ALLEGRO

My sister prefers happy, up-tempo songs, and why not? There's enough sadness our in our shared memories. When I sold the farmhouse I went up into the attic for the first time in years and pushed open the tiny cobweb-covered window at the far end to look over the land which had once belonged to us.

I mapped a path of sorrow from my vantage point. The most difficult year. A long hard winter was followed by a summer drought. We might have made it if a fire hadn't taken out the back field and spread to the barn. Uncle Chet's voice boomed as he rushed in to save the horses, tried - but failed - to hustle the pigs to safety. Men formed a line, passing buckets of water hand over hand towards the barn but there was nothing to be done. It fell, taking much of the equipment, all the winter feed, and most of the market-ready hogs.

Uncle Chet lost his eyebrows, singed his beard. I remember Norma holding a blanket over him, and lifting a glass of water to his mouth. He scratched the back of his neck and she stood on her tip toes to get a better look. "Jes a spider bite," he said, scratching again. "A spider trying to git away from the flames. Must'a bin scairt, poor thing."

I was scared too. Before that night I'd never imagined my father crying or squeals of pigs being burned to death. In nightmares I still smell the flames that reached for the black hide of the sky and the smoke that stayed with us for years.

As my sister plays now, I see her again as she was that night, outside in her nightdress, her hair loose down her back, her arm around Uncle Chet.

V LARGO

Norma's performing slower songs now, melancholy tunes, a sign she's growing tired. I reach for the violin and she lets me take it from her. There is applause, from the staff, residents, visitors. A few call out for an encore but I shake my head no.

Maybe it is a form of abuse, my wanting - needing - to see my sister this way. These few moments we have when I take her hand and walk her down the hall to her bed on the locked ward, where I'll tuck her in and sit with her until she goes to sleep.

"Dorothy." Norma looks directly at me and I let myself believe she still shares my memories, that she plays the music for me as well as for herself. "Dorothy means gift from God."

I nod. "Yes," I say. "Gift from God."

"Chet chose the name."

"Uncle Chet? Chose my name?"

Notes towards Recovery

"Chet loved our baby. He jes loved her."

In the face of all we'd lost, no one thought about Uncle Chet's spider bite. Never a complainer, he said nothing for days, just started in with the clean up, rebuilding the barn. By then his neck was black and split wide open, oozing pus, although I assumed the doctor could make him well, so he'd come back from logging camp the following May, in time for my birthday, just like every year.

It must have been a brown recluse, the doctor said, a fiddleback, as if naming the creature could provide comfort.

"*Our* baby-? Norma-?"

But there's the last of her smile, fading as quickly as the echo of her final notes, and her next words are gibberish. 'Loxoscles. Reclusa.'

Fruits of the Nightshade Family:

Most of all you miss that moment last thing at night when he put his hand on the small of your back and said *goodnight, Mrs. Potato Head*. You used to believe that meant something, that so long as he briefly touched that curve at the base of your spine and whispered that silly nickname, you, your marriage, would make it. For eighteen years that ritual survived.

But this time when he is away 'on business' you go to the Farmer's market to buy a smooth vegetable, the colour of a week old bruise and discover you can't say its name, too close to hers. You move your hands around an empty space until they meet and you are cupping them together. Then you leave holding nothing, except the knowledge that this time you can't forgive him.

Notes towards Recovery

Step One: Add Tabasco to his Caesar, so much so that your eyes sting.

Pass it to him as soon as he walks through the door, as if you are welcoming him home, like a tv wife from the fifties. When he gags, wonder out loud how mistakes like this happen. *How can she live with herself when she's fucking another woman's husband?* Before he recovers his power of speech, continue. *I feel sorry for her. Who christens a daughter Eggberta?* Shake your head, as if he too is ridiculing the name.

Will you feel better? Maybe for an instant, maybe not even that. But he'll find it difficult to sleep (why should you be the only one to be exhausted every morning?) and it will get his attention, let him know that you no longer believe his denials and lies.

Who has an affair with a woman called Eggberta?

Step Two: Take control.

Make this affair different: make this time the last time he cheats on you. Admit to yourself that at some level you've always worried one day one of you would leave: it may as well be you, it may as well be now. Your freedom is your prize - it's all you'll get, accept that. Listen only to the advice you are given that you might find helpful. Hire a lawyer and learn enough of the lexicon (pededent lite, ex parte, bifurcated) to communicate, but expect nothing. There are words from the glossary you don't need to learn: party, relief, resolution. You will not win, there is no winning, but know that he has lost because he has lost you.

Step Three: Breathe.

You no longer need to tip toe across the eggshells, brush your hair just so, tone down your lipstick, read first the books he wants to talk about. Maybe you'll take up running, start training for a marathon. Or rediscover a hobby you abandoned years ago. Grow vegetables. Make pasta by hand and crush fresh tomatoes for sauce, squeezing the pulp and juice through your fingers. Start with one of those blank pages you love so much; write a list knowing he's not looking over your shoulder.

Know that you have to navigate a period of pain and there is no way to make it hurt less, no way to make the time go by any more quickly than the time goes by.

Continue to breathe.

Step Four: Balance.

Chop chillies and onions, even if they still make you cry.

Do not forget all the things he did that made you sad. But balance them with the happier memories.

Do you remember balance? That was you and your kid brother on the teeter-totter in the schoolyard forty years ago. They still exist, teeter-totters - next time you pass a playground and see a little girl on one end, imagine your daughter.

Step Five: Mourn the children you never had.

Step Six: Rejoice.

You do not have to fight for child support, make custody arrangements, remain civil, allow that woman to help raise your children. You can cut all ties.

Step Seven: Cut all ties.

Step Eight: Allow him to keep Bailey.

You've lost your night time foot warmer, your motivation to get up some mornings, the reason you went for two walks every day. Suddenly you can stay in bed on Saturday mornings, stay

Notes towards Recovery

inside on rainy days, leave for a weekend with no notice, move away.

Maybe she is allergic to dogs. Maybe she came with baggage that will challenge him, maybe some day in the future he'll feel stuck.

See again Step Four: Balance. Maybe he will marry her and have her children and they'll be happy. (You don't need to believe this, really, but you can feel proud of yourself for even pretending not to wish them ill.)

Step Nine: Delete.

All the emails, texts, saved phone messages. Have several glasses of wine and then be very brave: disappear all the photographs. That time is over. Now cull the shoeboxes of old snapshots, sticky with dust. If you can't name your then-friends, the location, or the approximate year, the photo is meaningless. It may come as a shock when you realize that you are not a reliable narrator of your own history. Conserve only the stories you wish to tell.

Don't read his Twitter feed or find her Facebook page. Buy tomatillos and jalapeños and make for your true friends the Mexican dishes he'd never eat.

Step Ten: Start knitting.

It's what your grandmother did. Afghan throws and mittens every Christmas and gifts for each baby and child at his or her birthday. A pale yellow sweater the year you were three, a green scarf when you were sixteen that you still wear. Now you understand what it means to have something to do with your hands, holding things, and holding them together.

(Don't look for a metaphor or missed opportunity - there was no way you could have knitted your relationship into something it wasn't.)

Step Eleven: Move away.

A new job, a new town, a new country where the morning air isn't heavy with the smell of woodsmoke. In a foreign place they speak of things that don't include you as half of a broken couple. Submerge yourself in the accents of strangers, the local slang, the names of villages. Stand in the queue at the greengrocer's market stall and ask for an aubergine. Smile when he teases you about your Canadian accent.

Step Twelve: Be open to possibilities.

When your new friend suggests a double date, laugh, but agree. Go on many such dates, knowing most of them will only be good for funny stories, later. But.

Step Twelve, continued:

Buy a new lipstick in your new favourite colour, goji berry bold. In telling stories from your past, confidently choose the memories worth sharing.

When he asks what he can cook for you, request his speciality, stuffed peppers.

There is a different rhythm to your life, you have forgotten what routines you thought you'd miss. (You don't miss them.)

Now. Listen. Tonight, just before you fall asleep, your head on his shoulder. *'I love you, Darling.'*

Congratulations. You have learned a new language.

And all it took was time.

Milk Rime

What I do remember: the sound of the crack in the ice and the eerie silence the morning after the blizzard.

That winter we skated all through the Christmas season. It was a year when the lake freezes all the way across on a single day with no hint of wind or snowfall - a thing that happens only once every seven years. At least, that's what I grew up believing, as I believed it was necessary to wear a hat in winter because eighty percent of all heat loss is through your head, and the Inuit had 52 different words for snow.

True or not that it happened this way every seventh year, that year it was magical: sixteen days of ice. (I stop myself from saying 'mirror smooth' because it never really was.) I don't recall that it was sixteen days, but I've heard the story so many times since, I often forget I was not yet six, too young to remember all the details. And yet-

I think I do. The ones that matter. Such distance, but if I pause I am right there: the metallic taste of cold air, the sharp sound of blades on ice, the smoke from bonfires dotting the shore, smoke that so permeated my snowsuit I carried the smell with me for the rest of the winter and into the fall, despite my mother's repeated

Notes towards Recovery

washing. That scent stayed with me until I grew up a size and I've no idea what my mother did with that suit; she might have been too embarrassed to send it to my younger cousin, smelling as it did.

Boys played hockey, using cow patties as pucks. It had been my job to collect the roundest, flattest, deepest-frozen ones from the fields in the weeks between frost and snow and even now when I'm out walking and pass cow dung I assess its worth as a puck. Everyone knew a famous or soon-to-be-famous hockey player who'd started his career this way; anyone could be next, though it was an accepted fact that the First Nation community who lived downriver from our town were the best skaters, best hockey players. Their reserve was on a bay which was the first to freeze over, sometimes as early as mid-November, and they were keen enough to shovel a rink, flood it if necessary, and keep it cleared all winter.

None of the town kids were allowed to skate on that rink because the bay was too dangerous. Too close to the unfrozen lake in fall, too close to the river that fed our lake as well, so often wide open with angry water. Once a kid skated off the edge, racing after the puck, and drowned, dragged under by the weight of his coat. Maybe that was only another myth - like the unexploded bombs in the cranberry bog, but it scared the mothers who scared their kids.

It wouldn't have affected me - their bay was far too far away. I walked to the end of our road and out on to the lake in front of town, where the big girls jumped and twirled, showing off fancy boot covers and matching hats and mittens, while the boys played their hockey games and the little kids like me just tried to get the hang of balancing and moving.

And the men - the factory closed, giving all the workers two weeks of holiday - I suppose they showed off just as much as everyone else. One afternoon Pa and another man were horsing around with an ax. How thick was the ice, who was stronger, who had worked harder that week, I don't know. Pa whacked the edge of the lake and, with a boom that must have echoed for a full minute, a thick black crack rushed across the ice, as far as we could see. Aaron was on the other side of the crack and I was scared that it would open up, grow into an uncrossable chasm, separating him forever from the rest of us. Boom. I remember that sound. Boom.

This was long before video games and all-day TV - when all the kids spent every day outside, but there are the usual indoor holiday memories too: putting up the tree and baking and studying the Wish Book, turning down the corners of all the pages with the most-wanted things. Even Ma turned over a corner - one in the home furnishings section, showing a happy family sitting in a living room with a three piece suite in pale green. The little girl had blonde ringlets and she and her mother were wearing matching red dresses. I wanted to be her, not me, with my brown hair in braids 'to keep you out of mischief' Ma said, though I never knew what she meant. That girl with her pierced ears - I knew it - would have bright white skates, and an ice dancing dress with pink and silver accessories. Not Aaron's old dark hockey skates, with an extra pair of thick socks to make my feet drown inside them a little less.

But as soon as I closed the Wish Book I forgot the white skates. I loved the bonfires glowing in the late afternoons and the ice etched with scrolls and listening to the big kids bragging about how far they'd gone. Miles. Miles. It was the biggest skating rink in the country. Probably the world. As my world comprised Ma and Pa and my hero, my big brother Aaron - I didn't understand a mile. After the ax incident Pa and his friends skated past the middle of the lake, five, maybe six miles they guessed, so far that

Notes towards Recovery

I couldn't see them anymore and I cried, my mother says, until they came back into view. There was talk, then, of a day spent crossing the lake, all the way to Quebec and back, but I don't believe that ever got past the planning stage.

It was Aaron who taught me to skate properly. I held on to the blade of his hockey stick and we set off, one push at a time, and he pulled me along until I was steady on the two thin blades, then he held my mittened-hands in his and slowly skated backwards. Ma says I was skating by myself at the end of the fifth day. Remarkable she says, the patience. I'm not sure if she is referring to mine or my brother's. Maybe both.

Without his hands I fell, I fell often, but laughed and got up and skated on, chasing after him and his big kid friends, trying to catch up to them, to him. This is the story my mother tells me now, how he only ever skated a short distance out of reach, letting me catch him as often as not. Remember, she says of our childhood. Remember. The first a question, the second an order.

I do, I always answer, even if that's a lie. I do.

There's a single photograph of the two of us on the lake, carefully posed. Christmas afternoon: Aaron wearing his favourite present, the oversized blue and white Toronto Maple Leafs hockey sweater, standing next to me on the grey ice, his right arm slung over my much lower shoulder, his left hand gripping his hockey stick, his face a study in teenage nonchalance. My big grin shows the gap where I'd fallen two days earlier as I stumbled from ice to shore, my blades catching in the crusty snow, my first two baby teeth vanished and unrecoverable against the white. (I cried, thinking the tooth fairy wouldn't visit. But Aaron dried my tears, told me he'd write a note to the fairy, not to worry I'd get two shiny dimes. And I did, the twin bluenoses tucked under my pillow to greet me on Christmas Eve morning.)

Another photograph, that morning: Ma on the pale green sofa. The first matching suite she'd ever owned, it was the biggest, most extravagant present Pa had ever bought her. We hadn't been allowed to sit on it that morning until she'd put down towels, and no food, no drinks, no crayons, no pens - the sofa and chairs arrived with a long list of rules, every one of which started with the word no.

It was Boxing Day when Dwight showed up. We saw him coming from far off, must have known he was a kid from the reserve from the way he skated, elegant and confident at the same time. We would have watched as he didn't slow at the crack but jumped right over it and into the middle of a hockey game, stealing the puck and scoring a goal in seconds.

That was the moment I lost my brother. From then on Aaron was only interested in skating with Dwight, imitating his movements, begging him to teach him trick shots. He even lent him his brand new Leafs shirt. Never before had I had to compete for my brother's attention, never before had the ten years between us been so evident. He had always shared everything with me, let me hang around with all his friends, but Dwight was different. They became a team of two, taking on everyone else and started speaking in a short-form slang I couldn't translate.

By New Year's Day I was tired, worn out from the weeks of excitement plus a too-late night and too-early morning, and feeling especially abandoned. I fell a dozen times, and gave up. My snowsuit kept me warm enough but it didn't have padding able to compete with the ice, hard as the tarmac that had scraped layers of skin from my bare legs the past summer when, against Ma's instructions, Aaron taught me to ride a bicycle without training wheels.

I told Ma I was going home to use the toilet, and would be right back, but when I had taken off my snowsuit I took two

Notes towards Recovery

baby oranges into the living room to eat in front of the Christmas tree, forgetting entirely about the new sofa. It was only when I stood up that I noticed all the juice that had dripped on to the cushion when I peeled them. I rubbed at it with a wet cloth, but that didn't help.

Ma would be mad. Really mad.

She seldom got angry at us, but when she did she'd shout, grab our heads, entwine her fingers in our hair, and bang our heads together. (This was an era when spanking children was accepted as the norm.) The bicycle incident only earned us a shouting - though praise and an ice cream cone two days later, when Aaron took off the newly attached training wheels and I rode all the way down the street and back without a wobble.

We had merited a head bashing that summer. The day before our holiday, a drive out West to a family reunion, Aaron and I were fooling around in the back of the station wagon, all packed and ready for an early morning start. I suppose Ma had done a last minute shop for en route picnic supplies. In any event, my brother and I managed to break two cartons of eggs without noticing and then kept on playing on until every scrap of white and yolk had slithered its way across suitcases and the car's carpeted floor. By the time we realized what we'd done, or perhaps Ma came looking for the groceries, the eggs had cooked themselves into every nook and cranny of the car, the cases, the camping equipment. I can feel her fingers gathering my hair, knocking my skull to my brother's.

The clearest detail of that incident my memory chooses to retain - there could be no photograph: Ma, having stripped down to her bra and panties, is hosing out the car in the driveway. In the background, the tent hangs from the washing line. I see Pa walking home from work as he does every evening at twenty to six, forty minutes after the factory's whistle blew, shocked by his wife's behaviour and hustling her inside before any neighbours see her half-naked.

She was tired the next morning when we set off. She must have stayed up all night to wash and dry all the clothes and camping equipment, re-folding, re-packing. For the duration of the holiday the car smelled as rank and sulphuric as the hot springs we stopped to visit. "Last one in is a rotten egg!" Aaron shouted every time we raced for the water, both of us cracking up at the joke.

Making a mess on her brand new sofa cushion, that was worth a head-bashing. Nowhere to go but back down the road to the lake, to hide from her anger for as long as possible. I took the cushion with me in my school knapsack, thinking - thinking- who knows what I was thinking? Maybe I was going to confess. Maybe I planned to hide it. But on the way to the lakeshore I passed Ma and Pa going home and they smiled, and I smiled, and I said nothing.

When I got there Dwight was leaving, heading home in the last of the light, and everyone else was gathered around the bonfire; only Aaron was out on the ice. He said he needed me to skate with him and at first I said it hurt too much, I didn't like it anymore, I wasn't any good, I had a big bruise on my bum. But he asked me what was in my knapsack and when I showed him he said perfect, the solution and tied it around me with the belt from my snowsuit.

"Try falling now!" he urged and so I did, sitting back and landing with a gentle poof. It was so much fun I fell again, and once more, and then we set off, him dashing ahead and me chasing, both of us laughing. I remember the laughter. The entire lake to ourselves and the laughter. And we had the last of the fire to ourselves too at the very end of the day, so we stood close, turning like hotdogs to toast both font and back.

Notes towards Recovery

It was only as we started up the road home he noticed what I'd done - what had happened - to the cushion. Ripped, stained with far more than peanut butter and jelly, holes burned into it from flying ash, it was no longer pale green but grey and black. All its newness gone away. He untied it and held it out and we both knew this was the worst thing we'd ever done, worse than the eggs, worse even than losing Pa's wallet as we'd once managed to do.

"Ruined," I said. I too scared to think about crying. "What can we do?"

"Run away," Aaron said. "Skate all the way to the end of the lake."

I've no idea what possessed him to suggest that, but I trusted him and followed him back on to the ice, not complaining when I stumbled in the dark, or when my legs grew so tired I could barely move them. On we went, past the marina, past the public swimming beach, until I saw the lights of Robillard Pulp and Paper coming into view. I knew we'd truly run away by then, that was where Pa worked, a bus ride away from town.

We had to stop we we'd passed the plant. It was too dark to skate on and it was starting to snow. I was cold, I was hungry, I told Aaron. Haven't we run away enough, I asked.

We made our way towards some flickering lights where, Aaron said, there must be people. First we passed a cluster of fishing huts, then the ice went on a bit farther than I expected and I got scared again, worried that we'd got turned around and were heading the wrong way across the lake. But it was just the bay; the lights were those of the community where Dwight lived. Had this in fact been Aaron's plan all along? He knew where to go, found Dwight quick enough, and space was made for us at the dinner table, the fish dinner shared out on to two extra plates.

We were lucky we turned in to the shore. The weather turned and the snowfall became a blizzard with winds that took down telephone poles and knocked out the power. Dwight's father went outside to get wood for the fire, came back in and said we'd have to stay the night, he'd drive us home in the morning.

And in the morning, the silence. That thick silence. Eerie. More fish for breakfast, and then we went outside to a new place, a world fresh and transformed. Every branch, every twig, every needle covered with inches of bright white possibility. The largest skating rink in the world was gone, and all the yards in the street were blanketed over. We were driven back to town through white tunnels of snow, in a pickup that had no seat belts in the back. Aaron and Dwight up front with the father, the mother and three girls and me in the back. What I didn't know as we drove through the magical landscape was how the friendship between Aaron and Dwight would last beyond the holidays. How Aaron would lie to my parents about after school clubs and band practice and pick up hockey games to come back here. How the two boys would hunt and fish together. How much - but how little - this boy and Aaron had in common.

But all that was to come. Then, I was being driven through a town so transfigured that I didn't recognize our house until Pa stumbled out the door, equally changed. This too I didn't understand until many years later. When the snowfall became the blizzard visibility narrowed down to a few feet and there's no way we would have found our way off the lake. Then the temperature dropped and, had we been outside, we would have died. The police had been called, searched by snowmobile with lights and gone out again at dawn with dogs. But they had assumed the worst, warned our parents to prepare for bad news. Ma had been medicated and when we arrived home and Pa came towards us he was crying - something I had never before seen.

Notes towards Recovery

The missing, ruined cushion, the catalyst for our running away, was never mentioned.

They quizzed me, then, and later, and later still when Aaron had his first accident. But I couldn't help, I had no answers. Had Aaron eaten a lot of fish? I didn't like fish, had I eaten less? I couldn't remember. Had he fallen and hurt his head when he half-carried me when my legs couldn't skate any further? I couldn't remember.

By the time I turned eight, it was clear something had happened. His walk was odd, sort of a lopsided lurch, and he started to slur his words. Then he fell on the way to school; the school bus driver who witnessed the accident said his legs had just crumpled, he'd flopped and gone down. The doctors asked if he'd been hit in the head, with a hockey puck maybe, and I believe Ma never forgave herself for the way she'd tried to knock some sense into us, certainly she never did it again.

The following year the school put him into the annex, out back of the main building. Poor Ma. So many of my childhood memories are of her as emotionally distant, sad at what she saw as the loss of Aaron's future, for which she always blamed herself. But he was my hero then, he is my hero still.

This year the conditions are right: the lake froze over on a day with no hint of wind, no snowfall then or later. Yesterday evening Ma rang to tell me the schoolchildren were out skating. "What fun we had that Christmas you were five," she said. "Remember? Remember."

"I do," I said. "I do."

So I've taken today off work and have driven up north, stopping just before town at the site of the abandoned reserve. The bay has vanished, replaced with an alder-filled swamp, unnavigable in any season. Impossible to imagine the ice, the fish huts, the skating. Up the road is the plant, long closed. Pa joined the protest, carrying a placard calling for compensation, justice for job loss and payments to those suffering Minamata disease, then took a janitorial job at the high school.

I drive away from those haunted sites to my childhood home, where Aaron and Ma are waiting. I lace up his skates at the edge of the lake and give him the toe of a hockey stick to hold on to.

And we set off, one push at a time, and I hear the sharp sound of our blades, mapping our story across the ice.

Push

Pushing. Pushing up through- Thick green water, sludge, weeds, algae. Surfacing. Breathe, breathe. Focus.

Focus.

Her eyes are open. Aren't they?

"Here you are!" A young female voice.

Who's speaking? Where's here? There's no water. She tries to turn her head to make sense of her location, but can't twist her neck.

Opens her eyes wider. White plaster rose, chandelier. Her ceiling. Montreal.

"That was a bad one, but it's over now. Let's make you comfortable."

Not comfortable. Everything hurts, a dull ache. A whirring sound and the chair jerks up, forcing her into what's called a sitting position. She tries to shift. Can't.

Blankets are tucked around her legs. "There we go, Marie. Better now. And I have your meds. Would you like water or juice?"

Gabrielle. Giving her the illusion of choice. Two years ago, when she could still control her swallowing she should have refused medication and food. Too late now.

Notes towards Recovery

"Here's the pink one."

The one that causes the hallucinations. Caught in a fire, buried alive, drowning in mud. Terrified, then always coming back to discover she's not dead. If she could make herself understood, she'd tell this girl she'd prefer the dyskinesia.

"And here's the blue one. And some more orange juice to help you swallow."

But her head jerks at the wrong time. She feels liquid on her collarbone, a drop of it running from the soft cloth that wipes her mouth, her chin, her neck.

"Let's try that one again, shall we."

The drugs. Anti-nausea, anti-indigestion, antidepressants. She can't feel her throat swallow the pills, but the taste of the reconstituted concentrate lingers on her tongue. A brief sense of her mother's hands on hers as they squeezed oranges for juice.

Do her hands look like her mother's did at the end, paper thin and tinged with blue?

"Your hands? I heard that very clearly." A gentle touch. "Ooh, icy cold. Here, I'll give them a rub to warm them up."

Just as she used to rub her mother's hands and feet each morning. And every afternoon in the park she'd wrap her hands over her mother's around the thermos of hot chocolate as they watched the world. Her mother, when she could still speak, shared stories of harsh Maritime winters and thin boots stuffed with newspapers.

"Papers, was that? Would you like me to read you today's newspaper?"

No. But that word doesn't make it from her mind, through her throat and out into the room. Gabrielle has already gone in search of the newspaper, which she'll read cover to cover if she thinks that's what Marie desires. Kind, really. And it fills time.

She feels the drugs pulling her away from clarity.

Something she wanted to say.
Can't recall.
Her window of words, for today, is over.

Her eyes open. Dull, pre-dawn shadows. She's in the room they call her bedroom. Except it's not, not any more. Her sleigh bed with its soft mattress replaced by this narrow, hard hospital contraption. Her Edwardian side table displaced by the hoist. Her collection of vases bunched to one end of the mantlepiece to make room for rows of pill bottles.

Opens her eyes and watches light move across the wall. Late afternoon then, that's when this window catches the sun. Weekday or weekend? She listens for children on their way home from school and the start of rush hour traffic clogging up Westmount. Buses, horns. A jigsaw puzzle of sounds to piece together. And closer, two sets of footsteps.

"The rain's stopped and it looks lovely out there. Let's get you wrapped up and we'll go for a walk."

Wrapped up. The carers' euphemism for the hour-long process to transfer her from bed to electric chair via hoist, wheel her into the wet room for a sponge bath and force her body into clothes. Then move her outside by way of a series of ramps. The boneshakers, her mother had called them.

"I didn't catch that. Can you try again, please?"

She doesn't understand how it is that she has no idea when she's speaking aloud and no way to differentiate between words and nonsense sounds. The hoist swings her above the wheelchair and she sees the stain, notices one girl mouthing 'dry' to the other.

Her mother's wheelchair, stained with blood, sat in the front hall for three months after the police returned it. She left it where

Notes towards Recovery

it was until the day she walked into it, couldn't catch herself in time, and fell over. Knew she was lucky not to have broken a hip. She put it out on the curb by the trash and the next morning, long before the garbage men came, it was gone.

The girls take turns pushing her along the sidewalk towards Mount Royal. She knows this hill is hard work. They reach the pond and stop beside a bench, sit next to her and throw leftover cake to the ducks.

Just as she and her mother used to do, every afternoon. Isn't this nice, she always said, trying to make it sound as if they were the lucky ones, the pair who could afford to sit and relax while everyone else rushed by. Once, her mother answered her. "Not enough." She'd heard her, but hadn't known what to do with the words.

A child runs past, stops and looks up at her, runs off again. "Papa, l'avez-vous vu? La vieille dame bave comme un bébé."

Old? I'm sixty-three.

Gabrielle leans over and wipes the line of drool from her mouth. "So many ducks," she says. "Look at that beautiful black and white one. I wonder what it's called."

I was a partner in a law firm. My interests were antiques and gardening, never bird watching. Barrow's Goldeneye.

"Garrot d'Islande," says the other carer at the same time. Followed immediately by, "Sorry, I spoke over you. What is the name in English?"

But the two words won't come again.

So the carers talk about a movie, pretending the conversation includes her.

She isn't ungrateful. Lucky to be able to afford private care. In a home she'd be left in front of a television all day, no one would push her here to feel the sun on her face.

"We'll stop for groceries on the way home, shall we? What do you fancy for dinner?"

-pasta fagioli. She discovered it on Sicily. That walking holiday with . . she's lost his name. But the thick, rich soup, sweet with garlic and the seaside patio where they ate bowlful, after bowlful of it.

"Pâté? Sure." Something that can be puréed, fed to her by teaspoon, but she can't make the word 'pasta' clear enough to be understood.

Banging on the front door. Now they're coming for her; she won't fight, she always knew they'd find her guilty. No sound then, no protest.

"Shh, shh, it's OK. You've just had one of those nasty hallucinations."

Darkness. Disconcerting, this constant loss of time. Never knowing the hour or day or sometimes even the month.

"There aren't any police, you haven't murdered anyone." It's not a voice she recognizes. A new carer.

I'm sorry, I've forgotten your name.

"Emmeline, but everyone calls me Emmie."

Emmie. Would you be so kind as to plump my pillow?

"Of course I will!"

Lovely. Thank you. And it truly is.

"A conversation, what a treat. I'll plump your pillow for you any time, and do anything else you ask. I wish I could always understand you this well."

But it's plain from Emmie's face that the next words are just a jumble. The clear speech, an after-effect of the hallucination, has worn off. She wishes she could close her eyes and curl into her pillow.

Notes towards Recovery

Pillows. At some point it had stopped being a joke when her mother begged her to put a pillow over her face and it had ceased to scare her that she took her mother's requests seriously. But they had filled the evenings watching murder mysteries on television, and they both knew that murder by smothering left too many clues. A face imprint, skin cells.

Wakes to: "The first snowfall! Let's go to the park." She's being hoisted, put into a winter coat, hat and gloves. The girls hurry. She knows why; any change in routine is exciting.

It was the same when she was the caregiver. Guess who's come to visit you? she'd ask her mother in a voice, artificial even to her own ears. As if the community health nurse, Mathis, was worth the fuss of finger sandwiches and homemade butter tarts on fine china. But he was their only visitor for weeks at a time and generous enough to spend an extra half hour chatting over tea. It was Mathis who took her aside to ask her about her own health although she insisted the shaking was caused by stress, exhaustion. Even in denial she was just like her mother.

The park is full of children. "I love this," says Emmie.

"I don't remember snow this early in the season when I was their age," says Gabrielle. She points. "Look at them all, Marie. Tobogganing and snowmen. So much fun to watch, eh?"

Not enough.

No response. Have they not heard her or has she not spoken? Or do they, too, think it's best to ignore the words?

"It's rare that a mother and child are both struck with Parkinson's," Mathis had said. "We don't even know if there's a genetic link. But please, consider a check up."

So she'd gone. But when the results came back she couldn't share them with her mother. As best she could, she'd hidden the stumbling, imbalance, moments when she froze. She hid her own medication and looked away from her mother's gaze.

"We came out so early we nearly forgot your morning meds," says Gabrielle. "Look, Emmie's bought us some hot chocolate. With whipped cream no less." She blows on it to cool it, then offers a tiny spoonful of cream with tablet. "Here you go. Good. One more. And, last one."

The last one. If only I could be sure it was.

"Have another sip. Isn't it lovely?"

Mother and I on this same bench, drinking hot chocolate. That day.

A small girl, blonde curls and bright pink snowsuit runs past, flops into the snow and waves her arms about. She jumps up, giggles at the shape she's left in the snow and dashes away.

"Shall we?" Emmie laughs. "I wonder what people would say if the three of us lay down in the snow and started making angels."

I'd like that.

"Would you?" Emmie turns to smile at her.

The drugs must have kicked in quickly. Her speech is strong and sure. This is her chance. Today, with the sun on the snow. Please, could push me up the Olmsted Trail?

"You want us to work off that hot chocolate and whipped cream, don't you?" Gabrielle says. "Sure, it'll be a great view from the top. We'll be able to see all of Montreal and along the Saint Laurent."

Emmie points to the sky. "Look at those clouds moving in. More snow, I bet. I hope this means we'll have a good ski season."

Hope. I live in hope.

"Oh. Marie." Emmie looks at her. "One day, you know. One day they'll find a cure for this shitty disease. God willing it will

Notes towards Recovery

be in your lifetime." She kneels to tuck the blankets around her. "And I saw from your photo albums that you were a skier. Me and my big mouth, I'm sorry."

Emmie has misunderstood. It's not a cure she's hoping for, or a day of skiing. Her chair's wheels slipping on the snow or a frozen patch on the shady sidewalk; a momentary loss of control.

A moment. That's all it was that day, between the holding of the handles and her mother's chair in the road, a car unable to swerve or stop.

That day.

Mathis had met her at the hospital, sat with her in the beige room when the doctors spoke to her, and again when the policewoman interviewed her. A tragic accident, Mathis said. Tragic, the policewoman agreed.

The medication is affecting her memory. She isn't sure. Was it just an icy patch? Had her hands started to shake uncontrollably? Or had she, perhaps- Was it possible she had given the wheelchair the merest touch of encouragement?

How about that view? she had asked her mother when they finally reached the top of the Olmsted. How about that?

"Enough," her mother had said. "Enough."

Northern Lights

You might not notice her if you were under the overhang, not exactly the regulation nine meters away from the building but out of the worst of the slanting sleet in order to light a smoke. She doesn't draw attention to herself; she's driven a small, older car which she has to park in the back row. The other drivers arrived several hours earlier and their cars are already coated with the morning's ice. She hunches into the wind as she navigates the slippery path to the entrance, clasping her hood around her chin with one hand, with the other holding her backpack to her front like an extra belly.

It's difficult to see her, features hidden by the fake fur which is already matting in the wet and body disguised by the knee-length down jacket. And it's a grey January day - slate sky, charcoal trees, even the red brick building looks smoky through the sleet. What you might think, even without realizing it, is that she too is grey. Nondescript. She lacks the authoritarian bearing of a staff member but nothing about her suggests a patient. No slightly off-kilter gait, no facial tics, no muttering to herself.

When the wind extinguishes your third match you'll focus on scrambling through your inside pocket for another book of matches, swearing at your lack of a lighter, and miss the nervous

Notes towards Recovery

smile she gives you as she walks by and pulls open the heavy doors. Finally, your first drag and before the doors have fully closed, you'll have forgotten all about her.

She pauses before the next set of double doors, and then she does whisper to herself. "Joy? Yes? I love you. Good." Several times a week this same conversation with herself, so close to a mantra that she barely hears the words as she thinks them. It started - she thinks it started - the summer she was fifteen. The end-of-season canoe trip, once her favourite part of summer camp. That was the year a gulf had appeared between her and every other girl her age; the books she read and games she played and clothes she wore were wrong. Everyone else in her cabin had moved on to dances and boys and Judy Blume, experimenting with French kissing and words Joy couldn't even translate. It was a three-week trip, right across the park. By lunch on the first day Joy knew it would be the longest three weeks of her life. (She was wrong about that. But.)

She tried to pretend, she canoed hard and carried more than her fair share over the portages, but this did nothing to bridge the gap. All the other girls were buddies with the counsellors, sharing cigarettes and contraband beer. To stem the tears, she whispered to herself when she was away from the group, gathering kindling or looking for blueberries. "I love you," she told herself. Some years later she started confirming that she'd heard herself. "Good," she'd say.

All the years since that summer, all the therapists and doctors and psychologists and she's never shared this tiny nugget of information about herself with anyone. She wonders sometimes if it could be a key, the key, the one thing that would unlock something, fix what it is that needs fixing. Thirty-two and she is still looking for a magic cure.

"Physician, heal thyself," Dan had joked when she told him about this new gig. She thinks - she hopes - he was joking. She laughed. But it is something she might actually be good at. And it pays, pays well. Comparatively.

So here she is, shaking off the worst of the snow, stamping her boots on the mat and unzipping her coat to show her staff badge to the security guard at the front desk. She signs in and he reaches under the counter to press the buzzer that will open the doors. Although she knows she can leave at any time, the sound they make as they click shut behind her makes her uneasy. She clutches her backpack and looks straight ahead.

It takes her a moment to remember she has to swipe her badge again to call the elevator, and once more inside to activate it. Maybe she'll take the stairs next time. Three flights twice a day, that would be good for her.

She's been asked to start each day by leading fifteen minutes of stretching exercises. Only three people take part, all the others watch from where they are slumped on sofas and in easy chairs. In the background the muted television plays a game show, someone spinning a wheel then jumping up and down. As Joy reaches above her head, behind her back, touches her toes, a janitor takes down the last of the Christmas decorations from the walls and squashes them into a plastic bin to make them fit. The room looks tired, and the dull light seeping into the room only illuminates the dust drifting towards the worn floor tiles. The whole ward appears to be settling in for the cold weather doldrums.

Her first group is Art Therapy. Easy. She's done this before and is well prepared with magazines and glue sticks to make collages. Vision boards, she calls them, what the future could hold. The men rip out pictures of expensive cars and skinny bikini-clad models, the women choose houses with neat-as-a-pin kitchens

Notes towards Recovery

and tables with a good-looking family tucking into a roast turkey dinner, or women in groups in spas or lunching in expensive cafés, or the same skinny models as the men. No one chooses a picture of a newborn baby. The two hours pass without incident and then the Tea Lady comes through the common room pushing a trolley with lukewarm drinks and saran-wrapped rice krispie squares. Clearly the highlight of the morning.

Then the real challenge, facilitating the peer support session. That's the title of this job: Peer Support Facilitator. She spent hours looking up websites for structured plans and ideas, came away with little. The room is at the other end of the floor, away from the noise of the television; two sets of double doors to be unlocked and then locked behind them. It's pale green and dull. Three lamps on empty bookcases cast only the suggestion of light. She fusses a bit with the hard plastic chairs, making as friendly a circle as she can in the limited space. One of the women helps while she finishes eating, her marshmallow-sticky fingers marking the back of each of the chairs she moves.

"Good morning," says Joy. She chooses a non-sticky chair and smiles. "I'm Joy." She had stood, walked around the room, for the art therapy session. Now, sitting, she sees how ill-fitting this navy suit is. Bought from Walmart last night in a sudden panic that the baggy sweaters and elasticated skirts she owned wouldn't look professional enough. The cheap pants bunch at her waist, stretch across her thighs, and the sleeves of the jacket reach to her knuckles. "Perhaps you could introduce yourselves to me and each other?"

A silence; she should have prepared a more formal ice breaker. Finally the woman scrunching saran wrap into a ball, wiping her hands on her jeans, meets Joy's gaze. She half-stands, hesitates, sits again. "Hello. My name is Chardonnay and I'm an alcoholic."

"Hello, Chardonnay." This from everyone in the room. The woman relaxes.

Joy keeps what she hopes is an encouraging smile on her face. She signed several forms, ticked the data protection box, but she may tell Dan about the alcoholic whose parents saw fit to name her after a kind of wine. "And what would you like to talk about today?"

"I need to look at the guilt and loneliness that makes me want to lapse backwards. I have suffered from the disease of alcoholism. There is no disgrace in facing up to the fact that I have a problem, but I know if I do not drink today I cannot get drunk today." She nods, as if pleased with the answer she's given. Quoted word-for-word. Joy has read all the AA Pamphlets in waiting rooms over the years.

How long until her smile starts to fade? She thanks the woman for her honesty, then looks towards the man on Chardonnay's right. "Hello. You are-?"

"Jesus."

"No he's not. He's Kenny." This from an older man across the circle.

"I'm happy to call you Jesus if that's the name you prefer," says Joy. Is that what she's supposed to do? Or is it more helpful to use the name mainstream society will use when Jesus . . Kenny is released? "Are there any specific issues you'd like to raise in this group?" she asks.

He shakes his head. "Hate talkin'. Only here 'cause I have no choice."

Friendly, open, but no pressure. She knows this much. "Well, I'm glad you're here and if you choose to join in we'd love you to." Should she be using a more professional-sounding jargon, or would it sound as fake to them as it always did to her? How

Notes towards Recovery

to communicate. She thinks about the lack of communication between her and Dan. Lack of effective communication.

After three more people decline her offer to share, to talk about anything at all, she says, "Communication is always about choices." So easy to suggest. She runs through a list of techniques she'd never dare suggest to Dan that they might try, even though she knows she'll arrive home to the breakfast dishes unwashed and no sign of supper despite it being his day off. He has other strengths, she reminds herself, she could list them by rote as she often does to her mother. He is kind. Generous. He has a job. He didn't leave her when many other men would have.

And communication isn't one of her strengths either. Far easier to cook dinner and wash the dishes and then watch television together.

They reach the man who busted Jesus. Andrew. She thinks she might recognize him, she isn't sure. His first few sentences sound prepared, he wants to discuss the problems he's having sleeping next to someone who snores, and how he's only allowed four smoke breaks a day and that's not enough. But then he starts to ramble, launching into a story about travelling through northern B. C. "back when I was well," and hitchhiking across the border into Alaska.

Joy should probably rein him in, move the discussion on to other topics. But he's enjoying the reminiscing and no one else seems to mind and - she's completely out of her depth. There is nothing real she can offer these people; listening might be the best she can do.

"-and the salmon. You should'a seen them salmon." He winds up his travelogue by holding his hands about four and a half feet apart.

"It sounds like you have lots of good memories from that time in your life," says Joy. "Who else would like to share some good memories?"

Chardonnay holds up her hand. "I suffer from false memories oftentimes," she says, "as a result of when I was drinking I thought I was the life of the party and had friends and good times, but looking back I know that wasn't me at all but what the alcohol I drank made me into. They weren't my real friends and when the chips were down and I needed to lean on people for support that's when I looked up and there was no one there."

"And do you have good friends to support you now?" asks Joy.

Chardonnay nods, gestures around the room. "You cannot pick your family, I learned that, but you can make a family around you from friends and that's what I've done here with these good folks."

"I am not your family," Jesus mutters. "And I hate salmon."

"What about moose?" Andrew asks. "I ate some good moose up there. Nothing like moose grilled over a campfire. And the sky, them things that light up the sky, whatcha call 'em."

"Stars?" offers a plump girl who must be eighteen but looks about twelve. Very soft voice, but helpful, no hint of sarcasm.

"Nah, more like lasers," says Andrew. "You'd love 'em, Char. All pretty colours, like being drunk but no booze, no hangover." He details an experience of watching the multi-coloured sky above a pine forest, the colours shifting and turning to silent music.

"The Northern Lights," says Joy. "You've described them beautifully."

"Wataway. Aurora Borealis," says Jesus.

"That's it," says Joy. "I'd forgotten the proper term. And I've never known what causes them."

Notes towards Recovery

"Our ancestor spirits dancing, forming a path to the next world for our souls." This from Jesus.

Joy blinks. Thinks of her baby dancing through the sky.

"You could look it up on the internet," says Chardonnay. "There is no disgrace in admitting you do not know something. You have the power to choose what you change about your life situation and acquiring knowledge is a source of power."

Joy pulls her cell phone from her coat pocket before she remembers there's no Wi-Fi here. "I'll make a note to do just that," she says, shoving her phone away and writing on the blank sheet of paper on her clipboard.

One of the other women watches her write. "Is that all you do? Look stuff up?" A pause. "You're not even a psychologist, are you?"

"No. No I'm not," said Joy. She's struggles to think of the woman's name, can't. "My job title is Peer Support Facilitator." The words sound even more ridiculous out loud than they looked on the contract.

"And what're you doing here?" the woman demands. Her voice is hard and her face suggests years of heavy drug abuse. "What training do you have to help us?"

Joy was expecting this question, had an answer ready which she'd practiced in the car as she drove in this morning but it would sound as phoney as her job title. "I need the cash," she says. "This pays. Better than part-time shifts at Tim Horton's and Canadian Tire, which is what I was doing over Christmas."

"Your coat is Mark's Work Wearhouse," says the teenage girl. "Did you get it free?"

"Not free, but I had a staff discount," Joy admits. "Twenty percent. On top of the markdown price because it's last season's colour."

"I think it's a pretty colour," says the girl.

"So you're not here for our sake. You have no experience." The hard woman again.

Joy chooses truth. "I was sick," she says. "And I got better. I guess they think that gives me something called lived experience." She notices she's put her hand on her stomach and pulls it back.

Andrew has finished coughing. He leans forward. "I was a rigger in Alberta, back in the boom days," he says. "Never held a tool in my hand before my first day on the job. Learnt more in one morning than days of book-reading in the classroom. Sometimes you just gotta do stuff to get the hang of it."

Joy smiles at the older man, grateful for his support. It's enough to give her a way in, and she finds herself leading a conversation about means of learning, how to think about making healthy choices. Everyone contributes at least one sentence. Useful? She couldn't say. But the following week Chardonnay will have a new set of slogans to parrot back, try to live by.

She catches herself staring at the teenager, and looks away. Overweight? Or starting to show? When she'd been pregnant - *thought she'd been pregnant*, she reminds herself in a tired tape-recording of a voice she doesn't believe, even now - whenever she'd seen another mother-to-be she always smiled, patting her own belly at the same time. She thought they'd been sharing congratulations, pride. Had she looked unhinged, even then?

The hour is over, which means standing, walking back the length of the hall through both sets of security doors - click. click. - to the common room where lunch will be served.

"I appreciate your honesty, Joy," says the hard woman, walking beside her. "Being here for a pay cheque an' all. That's rent, that's groceries."

She doesn't smile but Joy hears a hint of grace in the woman's voice. "Thank you," she says.

"You do know about Andrew, eh?" the woman continues.

Notes towards Recovery

Leslie. Her name is Leslie, Joy remembers. "Know about him?"

"All that bullshit about northern B. C. , Alaska, working the rigs in Edmonton. He's never been outside Sudbury city limits." Leslie snorts, walks ahead.

Caught off guard, Joy loses her balance, reaches to the wall to steady herself. Real or imagined, truth or fiction, does it matter?

Staff members are encouraged to eat with the patients, so she'll sit wherever there's a space for the mac and cheese, bread and margarine, lettuce with cucumber and tinned pears, served in a yellow plastic tray, some of the pear juice slopped over the edge of the compartment making the bread soggy.

This afternoon... she doesn't even know what she's leading, facilitating, this afternoon. Whatever it's called, she'll make it art therapy again. Black construction paper and pastels - they'll draw the Northern Lights and talk about things that shift, can't be pinned down and she'll ask Jesus to tell them more about the dancing spirits. It comes to her then, some memory of a high school science class, particles and atoms in the upper atmosphere, their colours a reflection of the sun. Maybe. She prefers the image of dancing.

When she gets home Dan will ask her about her day, and he'll listen to any details she chooses to share. She knows now she won't say much because these aren't her stories to tell.

She thinks of B. C. and Alaska and all the other places she's never been. The canals of Venice, the zig-zag hills of San Francisco, Walt Disney World, Legoland. Why shouldn't Andrew embellish if he wants to? She edits her life story every time - too often - she has to sit in a circle like that, paring back all but the most necessary details.

When the workday ends, in the late afternoon of darkness and cooling temperatures, and you go outside for your precious fourth smoke break of the day - too early, you'll be anxious after dinner when you're stuck inside - she passes you again. You hear her hacking at the ice which has blurred and rippled over the windshield, using one of those crap dollar store scrapers. Finally she starts the engine and lets it run, melting a patch on the window just big enough to peer through.

You've placed her now. She and some guy live out the other side of town in a trailer park you know. Not much to distinguish it from the other trailer parks on the outskirts of town but theirs borders the far end of the lake, that bit where it narrows into swamp, so it's got the made-up name of Waterside Haven. An on-site laundromat, and a barbecue area but not much else. No fitness room or pool. It's an older place, with uneven tarmac paths and poor lighting.

You wonder how her evening will play out, imagine her getting home and suggesting to her partner that they do something romantic, take a walk say, to look for the Northern Lights. You can hear his reply: one day up the hill and you're nuttier than they are. Or maybe not, maybe he doesn't use words like loony, crackers, bats. Maybe instead he just turns on the TV, shakes his head, no thanks.

She might go outside anyhow, stand away from the trailer and look up. On her own, invisible against the night sky, waiting. You've heard her whispering to herself all day. "Joy? Yes? I love you. Good."

A buzzer. Damn. Your last cigarette break until morning. No more time to think these crazy thoughts.

Turbulence

This morning she woke from a nightmare - she'd been staring out the airplane window at the turquoise sea when she'd felt salt grit her face. She'd reached her hand to - and through - the oval window, then felt her body being sucked from the plane. She isn't scared of flying, she's never been scared of flying, but all day she's unable to focus on her work, on the last-moment jobs she should complete, and guilt at leaving her colleagues a long list of urgent tasks is adding to her anxiety.

She gets home in time to shower and when she soaps her belly she lets the hot water hide a few tears. Packing the last of her hand baggage, she hesitates. Neither of them has called this holiday a make or break - not in those words. Marriage or separation. Separation or divorce. She holds a pair of shoes in either hand, weighing the options.

If you pack comfortable beige flats, you will go sightseeing
If you pack sexy black stilettos, you will go dancing

She hears the doorbell. "Lisa! Taxi's here." David's yelling up the stairs and she shoves one of the pairs of shoes into her bag,

Notes towards Recovery

zips it shut, slings it over her shoulder as she goes downstairs, outside, into the cab.

"Lousy weather, even for February. Hope you're heading south." She hasn't the energy to make small talk with the cabbie; he turns up his radio and eighties love songs compete with thunder to cover the silence.

Wet snow slants into the car and she tries to ignore the panic that's throwing multi-coloured spots in front of her eyes. Looking past the fat droplets carving paths down the window into the stormy dusk, she tries to ignore the speed of the windshield wipers and the depth of the puddles the car swashes through by making sure she's got her passport, money, essentials. She's left both guidebooks on her bedside table where they've been sitting, untouched, for a month. Damn.

"I'd like to see the sea lions," she says. It is the only thing she knows of Montevideo: sea lions. He's chosen Uruguay, somewhere he'd been taken as a child when his father worked in Argentina, or maybe Brazil. She remembers only one story - a big dog in dimly lit haberdashery.

He doesn't reply, gives no indication he's heard her. The cab hits a pothole, thunks against the pavement, and she grips his thigh. He's facing out his window, as if the skyline view from the Gardiner expressway is worthy of intense scrutiny.

They turn up the 427 and she sees lights of a plane heading towards the airport. A shiver and she clenches her hands together in her lap. Shakes. This isn't unease, it's worse. Fear. Turning back towards her window she closes her eyes, forces herself to take a deep breath and let it out as quietly as possible. Opens her eyes in time to see a line of lightning bisecting the sky.

When she gets out of the taxi she stumbles over the curb or slips on ice, falls and scrapes her hands, muddies her jeans. David helps her up, asks if she's okay, while the cabbie lifts the bags from the truck. She's okay, she says. It's what's she's been saying for the past eighteen months. She's okay, she'll be fine.

Together they negotiate their way to the check-in gate, skirting a mess of people awaiting news of a delayed charter flight. Before, he used to walk ahead and she had to keep up with him at a half-run, but now he reaches for her hand, keeps his pace slow. As they pass a glass wall she sees their reflection and is startled. A good-looking couple, off on holiday. She turns to him and smiles, for a moment, happy.

This is how they met: she smiled at him in an airport. Both on layovers between long-haul flights, they'd moved from the hard plastic row seats to a faux-pub with weak lager and overpriced cocktails, where she'd prattled on about how much she loved hours in a plane when no one could make demands on her time. (This is how long ago it was, there were no laptops or cell phones then.) She'd caressed the cover of a thick novel. All that time to yourself, all that time to read, she'd said. Only then had David admitted he was flying back from his father's funeral, would make the same trip in five weeks to relocate his mother to Toronto, yet again. Yet again, he'd said. The hard edge to his voice the only sign of his otherwise well-hidden grief.

If you flirt only for the duration of your layover,
you will never see him again
If you have a third cocktail and exchange your ticket for one on his flight,
you will sleep with him next week

They'd discovered flats at Yonge and Egg in common. We must shop in the same grocery store, she'd marvelled, and drink at the same bars. We must have passed each other in the street,

Notes towards Recovery

she added, wondering if some part of her brain, recognizing him, had prompted her first smile in his direction.

They exchanged numbers and when he called her the following night she said yes to dinner and, after the dinner, yes to sex. That first year every time they went out to a restaurant they chose a new cuisine. Regions of Europe and countries she'd barely heard of, they co-discovered exotic, bland, sometimes inedible, menus. His adventurous spirit extended to bed as well and in her infatuation she agreed to much.

And, of course, they travelled. Favourite destinations revisited, and places new to one or other or both. He spent his air miles on upgrades, and she kept a list of all the countries in the world, ticking them off as they visited. Years have passed since that smile, that airport, and never once has she been scared of flying. But now, looking beyond the reflection of them as a happy couple off on holiday, she scans the dark winter sky for a longer flash of lightning, heavier snow, hail, anything to delay the flight.

"David," she says when they reach the line up. "I'm scared."

A couple arrive right behind them, all Portuguese noise and laughter. They have too much hand luggage, big bags from Toys 'R Us and Mastermind. Lisa averts her eyes.

"Scared? Scared of what?"

"It's-," she barely believes she's about to say the words aloud and she lowers her voice so the laughing couple can't hear. "I had a premonition that this flight is going to crash."

"Don't be ridiculous." A touch impatient. Understandably.

She tries to explain her nightmare, though it's difficult to describe the Caribbean in terms of menace. "I'm serious. I'm worried this plane is going to go down. Please take me seriously, I've never said anything like this before."

His shakes his head, the merest movement. "But you have. And you were wrong then too."

"Was I?" She'd been so highly medicated, she only had his version of what she'd said. No proof.

"Don't. Lisa. Please don't."

"Don't what?" she hisses, aware the couple behind them is letting the space between them grow, not wanting to be infected with someone else's pre-holiday domestic. But he says nothing.

If in his silence you hear 'don't mention the operation'
you will feel sharp cramps in your abdomen
If in his silence you hear 'don't mention the baby'
you will feel a stabbing ache in your heart

"Next," from the counter. It's a blonde woman, who smiles at David because that's what women do, they smile at him, his good looks, his charm, his sense of humour.

He puts down the tickets and his passport, holds out her hand for hers. Fumbling, she spills her purse, kneels to pick it up, the lipstick and pen and house keys and pain killers. Standing again, she places her passport on the counter, but leaves her hand on top of it. "Sorry," she said when the blonde woman reaches for it. She looks at David. "No. I can't."

"Lisa. Honey. We're holding up the line."

She shakes her head. "I can't get on that plane. I can't."

He sighs, glances at the woman. "Give us a moment." Reaching for his bag with one hand, he pulls Lisa to the side with his other. "What is this really all about?"

"I told you. I'm convinced. This plane is going to crash."

"Unlikely." He tries again. "You didn't sleep well, you're tired."

"It's my instinct."

"And you trust it."

Notes towards Recovery

"I should. I should have learned by now-" She bites off the end of the sentence, snatches back the words before she can speak them aloud.

> *If you follow the doctor's recommendation for a*
> *medically based termination,*
> *you might save a child from a brief life of extreme pain*
> *If you choose to demand a third and fourth opinion,*
> *you might have a healthy baby*

She's not sure, she can never be sure, if she really did have that same shiver of unease moments before she was wheeled into the operating room, or if it's only with hindsight that she feels she ought to have been wary, ought to have asked for more tests. She wills herself to listen to David.

"You - we - need this holiday," he's saying. "Let's get on the plane, have a glass of wine and dinner then have a good rest. You love waking up in a new climate, a different time zone."

It's true. She does.

"And tomorrow morning we'll go find some sea lions for you," he says. "First thing after breakfast. Which will be excellent coffee with a fresh pastry, warm from the oven. Cafe con leche and bizcocho."

He knows her. Of course, after all these years, he knows her. Her stomach muscles unclench, just a fraction. He listens, he cares. If she says nothing more they'll check in, put their matching suit carriers on the conveyor belt and go and find two chairs in the Maple Leaf Lounge. She can look at a newspaper while he reads The Economist. On the plane they'll have a drink, two, and dinner, watching different movies but sharing the same air, same space. Then he'll sleep, and she'll doze through another movie, the earbuds falling away so there is only the tiny echo of sound wafting up from her lap.

It can be done. She'll ask him to tell her his childhood stories again. They'll make up the itinerary as they go along - walking the unfamiliar streets, visiting museums and beaches, drinking local red wine with dinner. If she stands here, perfectly still, she can imagine herself into a restaurant with a view. Feel his hand in hers as they explore some little town. Sitting next to him in a rental car, she'll put her bare feet up on the dash, follow the map with her finger as they wind their way to the coast. There must be a ferry over to Buenos Aires where they can spend the weekend pretending they're still in their twenties. It is the Rio de Plata, isn't it?

There. If she can name that estuary, she can do this. She nods, once.

Their spot in the line is gone, the blonde woman gives no indication that they can cut back in, so they go to the end, waiting behind a couple and their teens, all four of them staring at cell phones.

The Ria de Plata. River Plate. The River of Silver. A drowned river valley.

There's a rumble of thunder and the lights flicker. A collective gasp. She bites her lip and looks down at her hands, clutching her passport. Breathes, in and out, past the lump in her throat.

Worst case scenario, the plane does go down. Will they die before they hit the water or will they drown, their remains consumed by sharks? What if he manages to survive - if anyone survives it will be David - will he remember this conversation? She can still refuse to fly. And if the flight crashes without her on it what will she feel? Unbearable sorrow? Vindication? No. Relief. The thought, so clear, shocks her.

Notes towards Recovery

It's an effort to take two steps closer to the desk when the line moves. Does she trust her husband? Don't answer that, she warns herself. Say nothing.

If you'll do anything for your marriage, you will terminate this pregnancy
If you'll do anything for a baby, you will terminate this marriage

When they reach the desk she lets him swing both bags on to the scale, pick up both passports and boarding passes from the disinterested man. Follows him to security, answers the questions, takes off her shoes and watch and coat and empties her pockets.

In the lounge he pours them each a glass of wine and fills a ramekin with olives. She speaks. "If there is a crash, and I die but you survive, what will you miss most about me?"

"Not this crazy talk about premonitions," he says. He opens his magazine.

"For me it's the shared memories." She keeps her voice low. "Having no one to turn to and say 'remember when?' about one of the places we discovered together. A path we followed, a moment when no one else was there."

He turns the page with such force that it tears. "We're going on holiday to make new memories," he says, his voice barely audible. "Not re-hash old ones."

There is an announcement about their flight, the weather is causing delays.

She opens the paper, reads a headline about a multi-car pileup and closes her eyes before she can see the photograph, read about the fatalities. She can still refuse. Until she steps on the plane, in fact, until it has taken off, she can still refuse. There will be a fuss because her bag will have to be pulled. She plays out that scenario, hears his terse voice and the words he might say. It might be as simple as "are you sure, okay then, see you in two weeks." It might be as final as "are you sure, okay then, you've made up your mind." She could spend the time he was away packing her things and moving out.

She blinks herself back to reality, closes the newspaper, looks around the lounge. This is not the place to end their marriage. A last whispered argument is not what this past year and a half has been leading towards.

But her brief moment of courage, conviction that she can do this, has passed. This has no hope of being a successful holiday. The meals will be mostly silence, with patches of stilted conversation, between sips of the red wine. The sea lions, if they find them, will be dark blurry lumps through her tears. They won't break up while they're away but they're already broken.

If-
If-

Maybe it's not a premonition. Maybe she's hoping for a plane crash. She thinks of all the films she's watched and books she's read, all she really knows of plane crashes. Is there a warning? Or just a shudder and a falling away? In the movie version it would be a montage, a slow-motion of the crash juxtaposed over the happiest moments of their marriage.

The Portuguese-speaking couple arrive with two more bags, duty-free. Still laughing, as if determined that their holiday won't end until their plane touches down. They pile the bags of presents for their children in an alcove and head for the hot cheesy snacks. Lisa hears the neat snap as they open bottles of beer. That use to be us, she thinks, watching them sit with their backs to the room. Imagining the smell of their food makes her queasy. Phantom morning sickness.

Notes towards Recovery

The storm is over. There's an announcement apologizing for the delay, thanking them for their patience. A few more checks and they'll start boarding, please make your way to the gate, have your photo identification open at the picture page.

David stands. He's an Altitude member, super elite. This is how he upgrades them to business, why they're allowed to board as soon as the gates open. Get the best of the overhead storage, the pillows and blankets, the first glass of champagne.

Lisa remains seated. Considers her options.

If you stand, you will follow your husband and board the plane
If you were a different person, you would have risked carrying your baby
full term

Preservation

Valerie heard the door open and the sound of footsteps in sensible shoes, but she didn't acknowledge whoever was there, didn't turn away from her mother, still and silent in the hospital bed.

"Hello, Valerie."

She looked then. "Darlene."

"You look rough."

Was her older sister stating the obvious as a show of sympathy? If so, neither the tone of her voice nor her face made it apparent. Valerie ran her hand through her lank hair, imagined her eyes smudged with the crusty remains of days-old makeup. "I've been here for two days. I guess I probably do look rough." She heard her own voice, harsh and defensive.

"I'll stay with Mum." Darlene's voice was a little softer, maybe. "Why don't you go home, have a shower and get some sleep?"

Her sister's suggestion sounded like an order and Valerie's first instinct was to refuse to obey. Had it been different when they were children? As teenagers they'd clashed on a daily basis, as adults only grown farther apart. They worked at the same university now, and lived less than an hour's drive from each other. Yet they met only for holiday meals, more often than not at their mother's house.

Notes towards Recovery

"I'll call you if she wakes up."

"*When*. When she wakes up," said Valerie. She leaned closer to her mother, kissed her forehead. "Look, Mum. Darlene's here. She's going to visit with you for a while. I'll be back later. I love you. I love you, Mum." No hint her mother could hear her. To Darlene she said, "We're on page one-o-six," and placed the novel on the bedside table.

She stood, expecting her sister to take her place in the hard chair, but Darlene followed her into the hallway. "Valerie. I appreciate you're the more optimistic of the two of us, you always have been, but our mother has had two major strokes. She's been unresponsive since Wednesday. You have to know it's possible she won't recover."

Valerie shook her head. "She's strong. She'll get better." She pulled back her shoulders. "The spare room has always been ready for her and Michael's happy for her to move in with us."

"Valerie. No."

When had they stopped using the nicknames Val and Dar? "No what?"

"That's never going to happen."

"You think I'm incapable of caring for her." She winced at the accusation in her voice, then watched as her sister formed a smile that didn't quite reach her eyes. It was her gentle and patient look, one she'd often used when her children were young and one Valerie imagined she used to manage her staff at work. "If she is to recover, Mum won't be able to cope with your house. She'll need a stair-free home."

She was right. You're right. But Valerie couldn't say the words out loud. "What then? Her house has as many stairs as mine."

"I think we need to consider professional caregivers. In a setting that's specifically geared towards the elderly."

"A nursing home?" Maybe if it hadn't come out of nowhere, maybe if she wasn't so tired, Valerie wouldn't have been immediately opposed to the idea. But she shook her head. "I'm not dumping Mum in a nursing home."

"They're called assisted living communities these days."

"I don't care what they're called. I don't think-" She didn't know what she thought or didn't think. She looked down at the floor and wondered if anyone actually believed the oatmeal and blue speckled pattern matched the dull green walls, or if the rubber tiles only came in this colour. No doubt they were practical, safe, easy to clean and met all the necessary anti-bacteria, non-skid health and safety rules. But they were dingy, comfortless. "Were you going to consult me? Because it sounds like you've already decided."

"Why don't you go home and have that rest?" Darlene said. "I'll come round this afternoon and we can talk about it." Her gaze didn't meet Valerie's and Valerie guessed that Darlene had already visited a number of homes and narrowed the options down to two. She might suggest Valerie go and look at them, but really, the choice had been made.

Too tired to argue. "Whatever. I'll see you later."

She turned to go but Darlene touched her shoulder. "Listen Valerie. I heard about you and Michael... I'm sorry."

It was the genuine compassion in her sister's voice that made Valerie pause. She turned back. "Me and Michael?"

"Your... the separation." Darlene's voice was soft.

But Valerie shook her head. "We aren't separating. Why would you think that?"

"He- I-" Her sister looked genuinely confused. "He told me you've renovated. To sell, you know... "

Valerie didn't know. She could imagine some campus scuttlebutt, but she'd never imagined her sister paying any attention to gossip. "No. We have no plans to sell, nor to separate." She shook her head again. "If there are rumours, there's no truth to them. We're fine. Great. Happy. I'll - I'll see you later."

She stopped at the nurses' station and asked them to phone her if there was any change - any change at all - in her mother's health. As she navigated her way to the elevator that would take her down to the parking garage, she took a deep breath. Darlene would call, she trusted Darlene to call. They had nothing in common, they weren't friends, but Mum was their mother. As long as Mum was alive - Valerie didn't even want to finish thinking that sentence so clicked hard on her key chain as soon as the elevator doors opened. But she wasn't focusing - she pushed the wrong button and set off the car alarm; the shrill beeping ricocheted around the concrete space and she fumbled with the key chain for over a minute before she managed to stop the noise. Finally she opened the car door and sat.

Tears threatened, so "We're fine," she said again, aloud. "We're good," as she turned the key in the ignition, looked over her shoulder, started to drive slowly and carefully out onto the street and through a city that no longer looked familiar. Not even her own neighbourhood; an old hospital at the end of the street which had been demolished in the fall was now the subject of a police investigation and their cul-de-sac had been cordoned off. She had to park three blocks away and trudge back along the slush-covered sidewalk, hunched against the wind.

When she reached the tall, narrow house, she tried to remember the day she and Michael had moved in, full of plans to turn the dark, turn-of-the-century house into a light-filled family home. The big room at the top of the house was going to be a nursery, easy enough to add a dividing wall later so two children could each have a room of their own. But children hadn't happened, so instead they had added skylights, a bathroom and a seating area with views over their garden. A flat for her mother, when she was ready, for now a shared study although her desk had become a dumping ground for unread books, and Michael worked on campus. Research. The internet couldn't provide the first edition texts he needed, complete with authors' notes in the margins.

Why hadn't that first renovation sparked any rumours of selling the house, separation… or had she missed them? She walked up the uneven steps to the porch, counting as she went, kicked off her winter boots in the entryway and went all the way to the top floor, still counting. Forty-three. Forty-three steps from driveway to door. Exhausting. And it was Darlene, who had visited only twice since that disastrous Thanksgiving Dinner two years ago, who had been the one to notice all the steps.

Valerie ignored her desk, went back down a flight to the master room, considered curling up on the bed in her grandmother's quilt and falling asleep. But. Shower first. It took her some time to actually summon the energy to get undressed and turn on the taps but she did feel better afterwards, and resolved to go to the grocery store. She'd cook Michael a proper dinner tonight, homemade, with dessert.

She pulled on jeans and a shirt, left her hair loose to air dry, and went down to the kitchen in her sock feet. Finally completed last week, it still surprised her, thrilled her, every time she walked in. That she and Michael had such a gorgeous, modern room. Sleek stainless steel appliances, a built-in wine cooler, all set against cherry wood. She ran her hand along the polished stone countertop and onto the six burner gas stove then switched on the underfloor heating. A pile of takeaway menus in the middle of the island suggested that Michael hadn't done much cooking himself this week and the fridge was almost empty. Not even any milk.

Notes towards Recovery

Valerie found a one-sided flyer, turned it over and started writing a shopping list. Milk, supper - she opened the crisper drawer to see if there were any fruit or vegetables fit for more than the compost bin - and was greeted with the bitter scent of Seville oranges.

The marmalade. She had just finished the first boil when Darlene rang with news of their mother's stroke. There'd been no time to dig around the still un-organized cupboards for plastic containers, she'd just poured the contents of the jelly pan directly into the fridge before rushing to the hospital.

Now she carefully pulled out the drawer and put it on to the counter. This smell, the promise of sweet that was never quite delivered on, would always take her back to her childhood. Her mother had made marmalade every January, just as her own mother had done. As far back as Valerie could remember, she and Darlene had sat on the kitchen stools in their matching aprons and helped pit the fruit, weigh the sugar, write the labels. Later they sliced the oranges, arguing over the merits of a thicker or thinner cut.

Even though she and Michael rarely ate toast, rarely ate breakfast at all, every winter when she saw Sevilles in the store she bought them. There were jars of marmalade in the basement, rows of them, but Valerie gifted them and baked with them and kept up the annual three day ritual of canning the thick orange jelly.

Letting go. Not one of her strong points. She hung on to grudges, much as she disliked that trait. She clung to unrealized dreams too, well after she knew it would be healthier to move on. But making marmalade, this was harmless.

Her shopping list abandoned, she found the jelly pan where Michael had hidden it in the dishwasher, put it into the oversized sink and filled it with hot soapy water. For years she'd struggled to wash dishes in the little sink of their old kitchen; she tried to concentrate on how easy it was to use this one and she looked out the window to appreciate the light and the view, even if it was only dirty grey snow not entirely covering the remnants of last summer's unraked lawn. One of the magazines in the hospital waiting room had an article about living in the moment, suggesting just this - enjoy washing dishes, concentrate on the simple pleasures, seek out everyday moments of contentment. Valerie thought she could change. She would buy some of the fig cookies Darlene liked, or used to like, for when she came round later, and hear her out, agree to go and look at the assisted living communities with her sister. But first, this.

She didn't need the marmalade recipe but flipped through her box of three by five cards anyhow because the recipe was in her mother's handwriting. Her mother, who hadn't even seen the new kitchen yet. Valerie had invited her for Sunday dinner, planning a big reveal. But she'd had the first stroke on Friday afternoon and the weekend had been spent in hospital. And now- Valerie had to look at the calendar. Friday. It was Friday. Had been a week.

Valerie's stomach cramped at the idea that her mother might never see her new kitchen. As she poured in the water and peel she refused to let her mind complete that thought. She focused on squeezing the pits and pith from the muslin bag until it was dry, and the thick, clear pectin had oozed down into the pan. She wasn't going to be influenced by Darlene's pessimism. Lifting the pot on to the front burner, she positioned it with precision; transforming the orange peel and water into perfect jars of marmalade might be the single most important thing she could do to insure her mother's recovery. She lit the flame and watched the blue ring beneath the pot for a moment before going down to the basement to find a box of empty jars.

Notes towards Recovery

For the first time in years she forgot to duck as she went back up the stairs and her forehead caught the beam straight on. The pain was instant and she cried out, but managed to neither drop the box of glass nor lose her footing. Momentarily blinded, she blinked away the explosion of bright dots, swore once, and slowly walked, crouched, over the rest of the way. Getting rid of those damn beams had been high on her wish list, but one of the things she and Michael had just never got round to having changed. Bending had become instinctive. She'd thought.

She dabbed at her forehead with a tea towel; there were spots of blood on the worn cotton so she threw the towel into the back hall towards the laundry pile and started washing the jars. She'd always been a bit clumsy - Michael's first nickname for her was Flip, in reference to her tendency of tripping over uneven paving slabs, tree roots, curbs when they were out walking; those were days when they explored Toronto in an ever-widening circle from the campus grounds. They were professor and student then, and discussed CanLit, Northrop Frye, Callaghan and Ross and Laurence. Giddy with unspoken feelings, Valerie's care not to act on the urge to flirt rendered her even clumsier than usual and at some point most evenings Professor Keyes reached out his arm to steady her.

Later they strolled around this neighbourhood on summer evenings, holding hands and sharing detailed dreams for their future; then he called her Mrs Keyes. Over time the nicknames had changed to more generic terms of endearment and she supposed they exchanged them now without thinking. That same magazine in the hospital - she had read it cover to cover, twice, while awaiting news of her mother - had warned against allowing one's marriage to grow too comfortable.

They weren't too comfortable. She bit down on the thought. She and Michael were the exception that proved the rule.

The long-simmered attraction they'd masked until after she'd graduated resulted in a solid friendship, a strong foundation for a happily-ever-after for the confirmed bachelor and the much younger woman. The seventeen-year age gap, they promised each other, would never grow into an uncrossable chasm. Nor would the imbalance in their careers lead to an unmendable rift. They survived the inevitable whispers, her loss of the teaching job she'd hoped would lead to a tenure-track position at the University, their unexpected infertility.

Maybe this was the year she'd return to serious research. Back on track. And while the cost of the new kitchen would preclude a winter getaway they didn't need the excuse of a holiday to be together. Maybe, with this new kitchen, they'd even start entertaining again.

The jars were clean and dry, she put them in the oven to sterilise and rooted through the drawers of utensils to find the jam funnel and the dry goods cupboard to find the sugar. She couldn't remember how many oranges she'd used, she guessed ten. When the water came to a boil, sending the peel up to the surface in a series of eddies, she poured in ten pounds of sugar and glanced at her watch. An hour and a half. There would still be time to dash to the store for cookies, milk for Darlene and something simple, but home-made, for supper, maybe steak and baked potatoes.

Darlene. Valerie suddenly wondered if her sister might have called when she was in the shower. Their relationship was so fragile - she didn't want to ignore a call. Nothing on her cell. Leaving the marmalade on the stove she went into the living room to press play on the landline's answering machine. The sound of her own voice startled her - she was calling Michael yesterday to tell him she'd stay over again in case her mother woke up.

Notes towards Recovery

Then an unknown female. "Professor Keyes, it's Lucinda. I'm sorry - I think I've called the wrong number. I'll try your cell." Lucinda? Student, faculty, staff?

Then Michael's voice. "Welcome home, I guess, when you get this. Your cell isn't going to message so I'm assuming you're still in the hospital. I hope your mother is . . better. You might have forgotten I'm in Ottawa for the Symposium this weekend. Back Monday, when I think we should-" then the machine cut out, as was its wont.

Symposium. *Mystery and menace: survival of the heroine in contemporary Canadian novels.* He'd been invited to give a paper and sit on a panel. Yes, she had completely forgotten. So no need to cook dinner then; she could go back to the hospital. She wondered what he'd been about to say, what he thought they should do.

She picked up the phone to call him. Stood for some time, trying to decide what it was she needed to say, but she wasn't sure. She put the phone down and sat on the sofa, closed her eyes.

It was a hissing noise that woke her. Disoriented, it took some time for her to remember where she was, why, and to get to the kitchen where the marmalade was boiling over the top of the pot and spitting as it hit the open flame.

"No!" The brand new stove, covered. Already the heady citrus smell was overwhelmed by the stench of burning sugar. Valerie grabbed at the nearest handle, realizing how hot it was only as she touched it. She pulled back her hand, swearing, but she hadn't let go soon enough. Her palm was burnt, and in her haste she'd pulled the pot askew.

There was no time to reach for an oven glove or do anything more than back away and watch as the pot teetered on the edge of the stove, a wave of dark orange syrup swelling, then sloshing over the side. It seemed to hesitate; then, in slow motion, it fell. For an instant there was a waterfall of translucent liquid transformed into a stained glass window by the winter sun which caught each individual piece of amber peel in its spiralled dance.

There had been a moment during their wedding when she'd faltered, closed her eyes and prayed for a sign that her sister, who had boycotted the city hall ceremony, was wrong. She remembered opening her eyes just as sunlight entered the room, throwing up bright patterns which masked the dull walls, reminding her that all things were possible.

But it was only an instant - then the pot was bouncing once, twice, on the floor, spraying treacly liquid over the stove, the fridge, the walls and the cabinets, spreading across the floor, splattering her shirt and jeans, gumming into her hair. Boiling sugar - everywhere.

Valerie grabbed the cloth from the sink, barely registering the heat on her feet, knelt down and started trying to contain the flow to the kitchen floor. The cloth disintegrated and she pulled back her hand, her eyes smarting with the pain.

There was nothing she could do; she had to wait until the boiling sugar cooled enough for her to start mopping it up. She backed away, turned off the underfloor heating, stripped off her clothes then watched the mess start to coagulate. The wrinkles rippled as the jam started to solidify; it would have been a lovely set. She dipped a finger into a nearby puddle on the floor, blew softly, then licked it. Her mother, especially, would have loved it, just the right balance of sweet to tart.

She picked up the jelly pan, noticing only then that it had chipped the floor tile. Tears threatened. Her kitchen, already robbed of its new-ness. The stove would never again look pristine, and when it was moved out to be replaced in thirty

Notes towards Recovery

years' time, there would be pieces of dried peel so shrivelled as to be unidentifiable, stuck to the underside of the oven and in the corner, covered with inches of dust.

She cleaned, hard. Soapy water, floor cleaner, powdered cleanser. The dark wood of the cabinets had blistered where the marmalade had hit. The chipped tile would always catch the dirt and the grout, stained already, would rot, eventually lifting the tile until it had to be replaced with a new one that would never quite match.

She wondered if Michael would notice the damage, would comment if he did, or what a real estate agent might say. Or anyone watching her now, scrubbing the floor in her bra and panties, her palm raw from bleach on the burned skin.

Valerie blinked. No tears. It was spilled marmalade, that was all. A mess, but messes could be cleaned up. She could make the floor be not sticky. She could fix things with Darlene; she'd tell her sister that she'd been right. That there were forty-three steps, she'd counted them. She found an old toothbrush and tried treating the grout with more bleach, inch by inch. The kitchen could look like it had this morning, if she just scoured it enough.

The telephone rang.

Darlene? Or the hospital? Or Michael, calling back to finish his sentence?

Valerie let the telephone ring. Whoever it was could leave a message.

She started to hum then, louder, and louder still so that she wouldn't have to listen to a voice on the machine. Words trying to fill the empty room.

Notes towards Recovery

I: GRACE ANNE

It was easy for me to choose you from the list of people who replied to my advertisement for this free sofa. Even before I read your email - so polite - I had decided. You have the same name as my daughter.

I suppose I'd assumed our Grace might take this sofa off to university one day and we'd replace it with something more modern, but it's lasted well and I'm sure you'll enjoy many years with it.

It was the first piece of furniture my husband and I bought together when we moved into this house; the rest was an odd collection of handouts from our families and leftovers from our own student days. It was the most garish plaid (as you'll discover) but cut price, and so comfy: we took it home that same day. It's still as comfortable as ever and it's always been my favourite place to read.

We bought the silk in a little shop behind the Ottawa market where the salesman made us strong coffee and served us rose-flavoured sweets and it felt as if we'd left the country entirely. He charmed me into buying the silk even though I knew it wouldn't be heavy enough to withstand daily use. It didn't help that Milo

Notes towards Recovery

designated this as his favourite napping spot, scratching himself a patch in the middle of the sofa each afternoon, or that we put it right under the big window where the sun faded the deep cayenne to a dusty coral.

Recovering the sofa was on my list of things to get round to one day but I never fell in love with a more practical fabric like canvas or twill. Perhaps you'll have better luck. If so, remember to pre-wash and iron the material, then measure the sofa. Measure it again, and then one more time and don't forget to allow for shrinkage and seams. Better to have too much and make it slightly loose, you can always tuck bits away. That's what I did, but then again I am an expert at covering up mistakes and hiding the worst of a mess.

II: COMMUNITY CHURCH QUILTING BEE

When I placed an ad in our local paper I saw your appeal for supplies to make quilts for people affected by the recent ice storm and wonder if this might meet your requirements.

It is a project I started the winter I was pregnant. My great grandmother made the original quilt and though it was badly damaged it had sentimental value and I thought I could recover it. I soon discovered it was going to be as much (more) work than starting a new one. All the sewing had to be done by hand rather than machine and I wasn't good at the chain stitch or binding. I hadn't realized how many loose seams and missing pieces there were and struggled to match the original fabric.

I had forgotten all about it until last week when I emptied the back cupboard at the top of my basement stairs. The real estate agent has told me that repainting the house will make the difference between sale and no sale. She was kind enough to suggest some colours - misty cloud, frosted breeze, iced eggshell. When I got to Canadian Tire I confused all the weathers and in any event they looked the same, so I settled on one called off white. But I digress, you don't care about all this. I emptied out the cupboard and when I reached for a bag above my head it burst open and I was showered by scraps.

I briefly considered starting afresh, thinking it could be good busy work to fill the evenings and make me feel productive. But when I looked through the pastel blues and yellows and pinks, all I felt was abandoned, unfinished. And then I read about the work you do, your recovery quilts for the homeless; I know you will be able to complete what I did not.

III: GRANT

I have given away the furniture and taken everything I want from the house. It didn't amount to much but know that I am not leaving you all the rest to be spiteful. You'll be able to sort through it quickly, dispassionately. You always were better than me at letting go.

I found a shoebox of stuff you might enjoy looking through; mementoes we collected that summer we drove down to Niagara Falls. Remember? We were so broke we stayed in that tacky hotel on the American side, with its magic tickle fingers bed and the leaky whirlpool bath shaped like a champagne saucer.
Our one extravagance was the day in Hamilton, visiting the Warplane Heritage Museum where you spent hours talking to that elderly vet who'd flown a Hawker Hurricane during the Battle of Britain. He'd crashed, he said, been shot down in the English Channel and managed to swim ashore. You weren't entirely sure you believed him, but I did.

He showed us a pocket manual put out by the Air Ministry and the Canadian Legion War Services that detailed emergency landing procedures and airplane recovery. It was only thin; I read it cover to cover while you listened to him reminisce. Then we

Notes towards Recovery

toured the hangars with the Spitfire and the Firefly and the de Havilland and the aluminum Grumman plane with its wings that looked exactly like a canoe, and I tried to learn all their names because I wanted so much to share this interest of yours.

I quizzed you about that booklet, asked you if there was a companion to it with guidelines for saving the pilots. No, you said. You said it wasn't that a pilot's life was worth less than a Hurricane but there was sometimes a chance the plane would be found, could be repaired, or parts salvaged and re-used. There was never a chance for the pilot.

When the museum closed we pooled our change and treated ourselves to dinner at a sports bar. I don't remember but I assume we ordered a platter of buffalo wings with celery and blue cheese dip and a pitcher to share. We must have shared a second pitcher too; when you asked me what I dreamed of I told you: a child. But even I could never have imagined Grace's squinty left eye, her cowlick, her tiny fingers that grew into sticky hands always reaching for ours.

IV: TO THE NEXT OCCUPANT, BED 2, WARD B

This is for you, this Easter lily, for your empty bedside table. You've been allocated this bed, beside the window, at the end of the row, just as I was. You may not realize for a few days how lucky you are - but you can turn your face away from the other patients and that long, beige hallway with its locked door.

Outside there is a maple tree, the river. Spring is coming, soon you'll see the tiny red buds and then the bright green leaves. You'll hear a riffle when the ice melts, smell the tannin in the water, the sap in the tree as it rises and falls. That's all you get - a view of a single maple and the sound of the spring run-off. But you have the best view on this ward. Hold on to this thought.

I hope you won't be woken by howls of anguish, as I was. It took me hours to understand I was making that terrifying noise. Only twice before have I cried like that. The first time was the day my toddler and I found our missing cat in the middle of the street, not twelve yards from our front door. The muted mewing coming from a mess of rotting leaves confused me until I got close enough to see what it really was.

It was my wailing that frightened my husband outside, where he found me covering my daughter's eyes with one hand, and with the other trying to gather bones, fur, blood too stuck to the road to be moved. When he rang the vet she said it would take her an hour to reach us. I couldn't bear to watch, or listen to the pitiful whimpering Milo made as he died, breath by breath, but it was Grant who was brave enough to back our car down the driveway.

When he'd done what I couldn't, he hosed down the street, dug a grave in the back garden and we planted it with crocus bulbs. The late October sun softened the sharp edges of his face at first, but as the afternoon shadows lengthened and he drank his way into a forty-pounder of rye, that same sun aged him. I can still feel that light, weak and thin.

You will get well.

You'll never again buy pine-scented disinfectant and you may have nightmares about being locked on this ward, although recollections of your first days here will be vague. You'll have to experiment with various cocktails of drugs until one of them works, as much as it ever will, and you'll get tired of telling and retelling your story in talk therapy sessions until it feels like something that might once have happened to someone else. Your heart may never fully heal but, like a broken bone, it can mend, and that has to be good enough.

Notes towards Recovery

V: DR. JOSEPH

You were honest from our first meeting, and I thank you for that. You said a marriage can survive the death of a child, but many do not. Some couples, you said, recover enough to move on together. For months our friends assumed we had made it through the worst patch, were past the point of separation.

I did not forgive him. I do not forgive him. If he hadn't been tired, if he hadn't taken the shortcut along the concession road beside the river and skidded at the curve. If it hadn't been dark, been snowing so heavily-- If, if, if.

You tell me I am holding on to the anger because I cannot bear to face the sorrow. You suggest that until I allow myself to feel sad, I'll never truly recover. You've encouraged me to start by writing an account of that evening, the facts that I remember and because you are my last hope, I will try.

VI: NOTE TO SELF

You never know what you'll learn over the course of your life. Names of antique aircraft and Disney princesses, how to paint a wall and repair a quilt. I stood behind the build up of windswept slabs at the river's edge and through the squalls I watched the recovery operation. I learned that water absorbs the impact of the blast when dynamite is used to break a hole in the ice so the windows of a car, only feet below the surface, will not be blown out. Before the explosives there was a chainsaw, fishing augers, ice picks.

The divers wore dry suits and full face masks and were tethered to the shore by a harness that looked just like the one in Grace's booster seat. They used underwater flashlights, and I mapped their progress by the eerie blue glow.

The hydro poles were moved so the heavy duty crane could reach the water. I do not understand how ice thick enough to support that machinery couldn't support a car. When they finally got all the equipment organized it was so quick - only minutes until the car was being lifted out of the river and swung over onto the shore.

A local reporter shouted against the wind, asking a policeman was alcohol or speeding suspected, and was told no one was willing to speculate on the exact cause of the accident until the car had been analyzed. Black ice, the blizzard, bad luck were all mentioned. That and - of course - the good news, the excellent news, that the driver had survived, swimming up to the surface as the car sank, inching himself over the ice to shore on his stomach, raising the alarm. He was suffering from severe hypothermia, but he was alive.

Do the details matter? It was minus thirty-seven plus windchill. The water temperature was thirty-two point one eight. The marine diving unit reported visibility of five point six inches and an unexpectedly swift current. All these factors hampered the rescue efforts. I stood and watched for six hours before I understood that *rescue* referred only to the car, not to my baby, my Grace, belted into her seat in the back of the car with the child-proof doors.

Stained

She'd been fooled by the light, the full moon's reflection on the snow bright enough to be sunrise, and in her haste to get out of the house unseen by the neighbours she'd pulled on the wrong boots. An old pair, with worn treads, making her pre-dawn walk treacherous. The calendar says mid-March but it's still winter. Her breaths come out in white puffs and the sidewalk is icy so she walks slowly, head down, concentrating on each footstep rather than admiring the scenery because she is old enough to worry that a bad slip could result in a broken bone.

No destination, no deadline, her only ambition is to stop the spinning thoughts that plagued her as she lay awake in bed, and to slip out before being seen by anyone staring blurry-eyed from a bathroom or kitchen window. She should buy a dog. Exercising a pet is an acceptable reason for an older woman to walk at odd times of the day. But she's ready: her goal is a footpath that leads up the ski hill and along a gravel road to the Anglian cemetery where her mother is buried. If anyone asks.

She's not thinking of her mother right now, but her son, Don, whose birthday it is. It shouldn't be so different from every other day, but it is. Gail forces herself to take a deep breath and look up. Hoarfrost has encrusted each branch, transforming grey poplars

Notes towards Recovery

into antler coral. "Beautiful." She tries to inject some feeling into the word, knows she's failed.

She trudges up the hill where, twenty-five years ago, she taught Don snow-plows over the Christmas holiday by holding him between her legs. After the New Year he graduated to stem kristies and parallel turns and by March Break he wanted to joined the racing group, out-skiing her in months. She'd understood this was parenting - letting go again and again, but she hadn't realized how often she'd have to let go, or how far the definition of 'letting go' could stretch.

She stops to catch her breath, pretends to admire the view. A singe nod towards spring, some holes in the river have opened and re-frozen several times this week. The open water is black, and rising mist wreathes upwards, like smoke from a smouldering campfire. It should be mesmerizing, an Ansel Adams-like tableau. She waits for the beauty of the scene to touch her, until she feels the cold working its way through her coat and up through her boots.

She starts to plod on, when a movement in her peripheral vision makes her pause, lift her head. A brief impression of a blood brown sailing ship, listing towards the ski hill. A series of masts extending towards her, their tendrils of sail clinging like the last of the oak leaves to grey branches. Just the idea and then it's gone again, hidden by a sudden fog but it was so close to shore it could have touched her and she backs away, stumbling, falling.

She pushes herself up, brushes off the snow, and peers into the silence where she saw the ship.

Nothing.

But it must be there. Waiting.

She's read of the ships that reached the shores of Alaska and B. C. from Japan, years after the tsunami. But this one? Dredged up from the Bermuda triangle by a current, it could have slipped between Newfoundland and Nova Scotia into the Gulf of St. Lawrence, then along the St. Lawrence River rounding the Gaspé Peninsula, passing Quebec, passing Montreal, gliding into the Outaouais, the Rivere du Nord, up the Ottawa.

Gail maps the route in her mind, thinking of all the cities and towns and settlements those waterways pass. Someone would have seen the ship before she did. And the hydroelectric damns, the locks, the sluices. It's not improbable, that journey, it's impossible.

But she saw...

She saw something.

At a sharp noise she steps back, but it's only the crackle of birch branches in the cold, followed by a thud of snow. She waits, shivering, for the fog to clear and the sun to cast more light, but still there's nothing. Could a boat have moved on so quickly, so quietly? Gail makes her way back down the ski hill to the edge of the river. Deep blue ice, not water, and no sign of anything having cut its way through, only the weeks old tracks of a lone cross-country skier, two white lines bisecting the darkness.

There's no path beside the river, only a few footprints - dog or wolf - and the snow is deeper. She falls through the crust with each step, but forges on, round the rocky point and along to the bay with its cluster of shuttered summer cottages. In places the wind has pushed away enough snow to reveal the colourless sand beneath.

Still no sign of... the pirate ship is how she is thinking of it. She expects it to loom up at any moment. At the stream past Wicker's boathouse she stops. Water is moving beneath the frozen varnish and she doesn't trust it. Instead she goes inshore, back into the woods, to cross the stream where it narrows up the escarpment.

Notes towards Recovery

It's only when she finds an overturned blue bin, its contents spilling onto the road - Tim Horton's coffee cups, menus from the highway's pizza place, baked bean and tuna tins - that she realizes she's on Jim Anderson's property. If there's a lane out to the highway it hasn't been plowed or shovelled all winter. She walks past rusted vehicles, a pickup and two cars. One, devoid of a roof, is host to a scrawny bush, its leafless branches clawing up towards the sky.

She looks at the naked house, no siding over the insulation board, and a tacked on porch of bare plywood perched on cement blocks. When she notices Jim sitting on the porch, she raises a blue-gloved hand in greeting, and he nods in return. She hesitates, torn between turning around to go back or cutting through his yard to carry on. She pulls back her shoulders. Why should she care what the town's misfit thinks of her? And yet she can't now walk by without stopping a moment to be polite.

"Good morning, Jim." She looks directly into his eyes, avoiding the brick-red birthmark that colours his face, from neck to forehead. "I see you're a fellow early riser."

"Just got in," he says, rolling a cigarette. "Last smoke before bed." He lights a match, tosses it into a fire pit in the centre of the porch.

"Just got in? Are you working nights?" She can't imagine where. She didn't think he'd worked since High School, when he was a caddy at the golf club with Don. There was a car crash and he was badly injured. Months in the Ottawa hospital, years of physical rehab and, she understands, a life of disability cheques.

"Working?" He says the word slowly as if unsure how to work his tongue around the unfamiliar sound. "No. Out and about. You know."

She doesn't know. She doesn't have any idea what one would do 'out and about' in their small town after eleven o'clock at night when the sports bar and Tim Hortons both close. The closest twenty-four-hour trucker's tavern is thirty kilometres up the highway and Jim doesn't own a working vehicle, only those bits and pieces rusting away in the yard. She was aware he kept different hours to most of the community but she's never before wondered how.

"I'll make you a coffee," he says, and tilts his head towards a seat beside him. She navigates the uneven steps to the porch and lowers herself into the chair, clearly taken from a car, shifting to one side to avoid a spring coiling its way out through the knobbly fabric.

He goes inside, and she sees now the fire pit is made from an old washing machine drum, leans close to suck up some of its warmth. In the corner of the porch there's an orange blob; Gail narrows her eyes for a better look. It's a pumpkin, presumably put out last October. It must have liquified and then frozen; when it thaws it will be a pile of mush, leaving a stain on the blonde wood.

Jim emerges with a chipped once-white mug. She doesn't look too closely. "Thank you," she says, wrapping her hands around the heat.

He takes a drag of his cigarette and Gail wonders if the odour, a peculiar combination of sweet and harsh, could be a sign it's marijuana. Catching herself staring at the cigarette, she looks away, not wanting to be one of the people who only ever notices Jim's birthmark. She concentrates on the flames, white, yellow, orange, looking for a pattern that makes sense, then looks beyond the fire through the trees to the river. "I saw abandoned yacht. I don't suppose you saw it too?"

He shakes his head, no. But only to answer the question; no indication he thinks she's crazy.

Notes towards Recovery

She describes it, embellishing. Adding a skull and crossbones that could have been there, and the eerie sound of the wind through the ripped sails. She hears herself mixing metaphors and realizes she's become one of those lonely women who speaks to so few people that she overtalks with any hint of an audience.

Exactly like my mother.

That thought shocks her into silence.

Her mother has been dead for seven years, but Gail feels her discontentment on a regular basis. Disapproval at the way her son left her, then her husband. Displeasure at her choice to take early retirement rather than face the overwhelming challenges of the new school system and technical equipment she didn't understand. And if her mother could see her now, sitting in a filthy chair making conversation with a man who might well be high on pot, she would express her disquiet with an intense look.

Seven years, Gail thinks, and still I seek my mother's praise. She could ask Jim after his own mother, but instead takes another sip of the instant coffee, so as not to start another long monologue.

It wasn't only that her husband had left her, it was that he moved in with Clara Campbell. One of the Black Creek Campbells, her mother would have said. With a weakness for liquor she would have added. Clara's six years older than him, short and plump. Once, when she was in the library, Gail heard Clara's teenage daughter refer to 'Pops' and realized, with burning cheeks, that the girl was talking about her own husband. Ex-husband.

Some of Gail's friends have hinted that she's foolish to stay in the four-bedroom house with its white columns at the front door. (An entrance she uses only twice a year, to greet her book club members when it's her turn to host.) One evening, after three glasses of wine she blurted out the truth. "This is Don's childhood home. What if he comes back?" Because children do return home, she knows this from stories she reads.

Jim has rolled another cigarette. When he lights it up Gail takes a deep breath and is sure. It's mary jane. Pot. Whatever it's called these days. He offers it to her and she shakes her head, no. Too late she thinks she should have smiled.

When Don was caught with hard drugs in his car and spent the night in jail she told him he wouldn't get off so lightly after his next offence. Not under her roof, she said, he had to quit or leave home. She never imagined her husband would be so opposed to the ultimatum, or that Don would so calmly pack a rucksack and go.

She looks at Jim, meeting his gaze. "Did Don do a lot of drugs, back when you knew him?"

"Knew him?" Jim looks confused. "You make it sound like he's history."

"He could be. I often worry that he could be dead," says Gail. "I don't know."

Now Jim is studying her as if she has said something insane.

"Would you like to read his last letter?" says Jim. His voice is so casual Gail can't believe she's heard him correctly.

"A letter? From Don? Don writes you letters?"

Jim stands again. For five minutes, longer, he moves about inside. She imagines he throws little away, judging by this porch. Stacks of newspapers, a pile of lumber, a broken deck chair and the remains of a parasol. But when he comes out, he passes her an envelope, upside down.

She takes off her gloves, holds the envelope as if it's an artifact from a museum archive. There's a ring from a coffee mug and a scrawl in black ink: *You are three hours late for dinner! It's Thanksgiving! Do you want to be part of this family?* and she remembers that Jim has a sister, seemingly well-adjusted, happily married, working full time and raising two children. Reading that message feels as wrong as eavesdropping in the library stacks so she quickly turns over the envelope, almost crying at the sight of Don's handwriting, barely changed from his grade school days. She runs a finger across the slanted letters, pictures his hand holding a pen, looping the J, capitalizing the post code.

There's no return address in the upper left hand corner, but in the right a Canadian stamp with smeared postmark. That stamp was only issued a year ago, so if this letter came in this envelope (and why wouldn't it, Jim's hardly one to make more work for himself in an effort to hide her son's whereabouts) then it's recent. And he lives in Canada. He hasn't gone off to Australia or Scotland or any of the other places she's imagined over the years. Not even moved down to the States.

"He's here," she whispers. Here. Maybe even Ontario. Maybe she's shared a subway carriage with him in Toronto, walked past him on a street in Ottawa.

Inside, a single sheet of paper, his handwriting again, and words that seem especially unimaginative. Mention of a ball game, some lousy weather, someone called Pat. A child? Partner? Wife? No indication otherwise of marriage or family or job. Or any answers to the question that keeps her awake at night - why has he never come back?

His signature at the bottom of the page is almost illegible. She turns over the paper, expecting nothing, and finds a postscript. Say hi to the folks if you see them round town.

The folks! "Who does he mean?" she asks Jim, pointing. "Folks, he says."

Jim shrugs.

Gail reexamines the eleven short words. The folks? She can't remember him calling them anything other than Mom and Dad. Maybe to his friends they were the folks. Or is that a reference to his father and-. Does Don know about Clara? Could that teenage girl refer not only to her Pops but to her older Bro as well?

There are no more clues that she can decipher. He doesn't appear to be hiding, he simply doesn't want to be found. Not by her.

Gail reads the letter three more times, then tucks it back into the envelope, considers asking Jim if she can keep it, and if they meet each other often. But instead she hears her mother's voice. "Tell him I said Happy Birthday."

Jim doesn't sound shocked at her clipped tone. "Sure." He closes his eyes.

The man with the birthmark doesn't need to look at her, she realizes. He already sees her, and not as a retired teacher who sits on boards and volunteers for the community but as a bitter old woman who takes an invisible dog for a walk because she's so anxious about appearances.

Who made her this way, desperate to be noticed for the 'right' things or not noticed at all? She can't blame her mother for all the failures in her past, all the poor choices she's made.

"You get used to the silence, don't you," she says. "Living alone." She leans back in the chair. There's a hint of warmth in the morning sun now, as well as from the fire. "I would like to see Don again. If he ever comes to visit, will you tell him? I'd like to know what it was I did."

"What you did?" Jim's calm voice has grown softer. "He left town was all."

Not town, she thinks, with resentment. Me. She never left her mother, not all those years. What gave Don the right, - no, the courage, to leave her?

Jim holds out the joint. "Sure you don't want some?"

"I think I will. Thank you." She only coughs a little, and only with the first drag. Discovers that what they say is right, it does relax. "It wasn't really a ghost ship I saw, was it?"

"I'm guessing not," says Jim. "Sometimes we see what we need to see."

She looks over at him, notices how the dawn light has softened the port-wine stain, nods. A ship though. Why would her subconscious think she needed to see a ghost ship?

When they've finished sharing the cigarette, he flicks the butt into the fire pit. "Right."

She can't translate that single word comment. Isn't sure she wants to. Isn't sure what she wants or doesn't want. She could leave the house. Leave this town, like Don did. No need to stay here in case he comes home; if he wants to find her he will. "They've asked me to run for Chair of the Hospital Board." Jim is the first person she's telling, because she worried it would sound like bragging at book club, as if she was trying to be the heroine of her own life story. A role which she is woefully, inadequately equipped to play. "I don't know if it's an honour, or if they couldn't find anyone else," she says. "But I've decided, I'm going to say no."

If she looks to Jim for even a hint of approval, she will be disappointed. His head has fallen to one side, he's asleep.

Dispatches

15 September 1931
My Dear Wife Bella,
The Doctor said you needed a rest so I signed the papers for the government to pay for your care. He says the best thing for me to do is let the city doctors look after you. I did not understand I would not have the chance to see you off. It's Mr. Sampson down the school writing this out for me. Know this, I surely miss you.
with love from your devoted husband, Samuel Ernest Eaton

2 October 1931
My Dear Wife,
I know you took the baby's death hard, Bella, but the other kids need you back here. I got a surprise for you when you get home. I got Frank Lovell to install a water pump at the sink for you. No more hauling buckets up from the stream.
with love from your devoted husband, Samuel Ernest Eaton

Notes towards Recovery

5 October 1931
Dear Ma,
I bin good, Ma, I promise, I bin real good. I et all the peas and swept the floor and washed all the whole house. I prayed every night like you taught me and I scrubbed behind my ears. Da says you'll be home soon as you get fixed up good in that fancy city hospital. I wish I could come and visit you but I understand Da can't leave the farm and it's a long way to take the horses in to Toronto. Please come home this week. This is the longest letter I ever wrote in my life.
Samuel Junior

11 October 1931
My Dear Bella,
It's been the best part of a month and I was hoping you would find the time and spirits to write to me. Better still, come home. We've all got pretty handy round here with you gone and I think you'll find it an easier life when you come back.
with love from your devoted husband, Samuel, and your daughters, Catherine and Grace and your sons, Samuel Junior and baby Charlie

26 November 1931
My Darling Bella,
I'm just praying this reaches you and finds you in good health. Please come on home soon as you can, Bella. I need you.
with love from your devoted husband, Samuel Ernest Eaton

1 January 1932
For Mrs. Bella Eaton
I am truly sorry I ever signed those papers, Bella. I asked the Doctor to tell me where you are so I can come pick you up but he

says you got moved to a new place and he has no notion of where that might be. You got to be better now, surely. I worry you have taken to the city life or life of leisure and you aren't planning to come back to us. Please don't forget your children who miss their mother and your devoted husband, Samuel Ernest Eaton.

15 September 1932
Dear Mother,
It's been a year since you left us. Charlie says he don't recall your looks, but I boxed him round the ears and showed him the photo from your wedding day and he recalled soon enough. We all miss you so. I'll be graduating in June (did you know that Mr. Sampson left and Cath has been my teacher this year?) and I do pray that you'll be here for that date.
With love, your daughter, Gracie.

3 December 1932
Dear Wife Bella,
Our girl Catherine has taught me to rite, just as she teaches all the children down the schoolhouse. Our first born a teacher. Can you imagine? I tell her you would be as proud as I am. I know this is true. I pray for a word from you in reply.
yrs, Samuel Eaton

June 1932
Dear Mother,
I know Cath won't write to you herself because she worries that stress will trouble you, but I can not let the date of her wedding day pass without your knowing. She has been stepping out with Harris Simpson for all last winter and last night he met with Father in the front parlour, and, it transpired, asked his permission for

Notes towards Recovery

Cath's hand in marriage. They are planning a September wedding and we are all very excited.

Is this big news enough to bring you home?
With love, your daughter, Gracie

August 1932
Dear Ma,
Miss Vesta from the feed store been helping out. Da couldn't manage by himself and get the harvest in this season. Some nights she's here so late she stays over. I like her an all, but I wish it was you making those noises with Da like you used to.
Your son, Samuel Junior

Sept. 2 1932
Dear Mrs. Eaton,
I am hesitating with the writing of this letter but wish you to know, first and foremost, that I mean you no harm. I know my place and yours and you are Sam's lawfully wedded wife. It is of weddings about which I am writing to you. I enclose a cutting of the fabric Catherine chose for her wedding dress which I helped her sew. I know she will be missing you tomorrow, as will everyone in the church. I am comforting Sam best way I know how, and keeping your children clean and fed. I feel as if we might become friends when you get home. They sure are keeping you a long time in that hospital, I do hope the treatment takes soon.
With very best wishes for your full and speedy recovery,
Vesta Adcock

Third September 1932
Dear Bella,
I gave away our eldest today. I cried when she kissed her groom. He is a kind lad will treat her good. You were missed more than I got words to tell you.
yrs, Samuel Eaton

June 1933
Dear Bella,
I know it's been some time since you had a correspondence from me. I got disheartened that you have never once replied. But Vesta, that is Vesta Adcock, urges me to write and her advice is good. This is our news, and I do not lightly say it is 'our' news. Catherine Anne Simpson (her married name) has given birth to a girl. Gracie will enclose a note with the weight and such details. I want you to hear from me the name of our first grandchild: Bella Marie Simpson.
with congratulations and respect, Samuel Ernest Eaton

Dear Mother,
Baby Bella is such a doll! I wish we knew of someone with a camera to take a photograph but instead I have made you several sketches. She was a difficult birth, but the doctor says Cath will be fine. 7 pound 4 ounces.
Love, Grace

September 1942
Dear Mrs. Eaton,
 I do hope this address, the only one I have for you, is current. It will be a surprise for you to hear from me after all these years, no doubt, but it is with a heavy heart I write as I have sorrowful news to relate.

Notes towards Recovery

I believe you know that Samuel Junior is missing in action on some foreign land as Sam sent you that news last month. Tuesday last we received a telegram informing us of the death of Charlie. I guess your memory of your youngest is a chubby lad but he grew into a fine young man and when war was announced he lied about his age in order to enlist and was sent to fight overseas. The telegram states he was a brave man. You would truly be proud of him. As we are.

This news, in addition to the lack of news about his eldest son, caused severe distress to Sam and his heart took it bad. He is in hospital and we are all praying for his recovery, as well, as we always do, for yours.
With deep condolences on the loss of your son,
Vesta

18th August, 1942
France
Dear Mother,
You may not even remember you had a boy who was just a child when you got taken away, but I have never forgotten you through all these years of your silence. If you read the newspapers much or listen to the radio you'll know about our role in this war. Tomorrow I head to the front and I am taking with me a Bible and the wedding portrait of you and Da. I don't know why I feel compelled to write to you, but war makes a man do strange things. Wherever you are, Mother, I hope you are well.
Your devoted son, Charles Ernest Eaton

***

March 13, 1946
My most beloved,

I truly believed when you came home from that war, the worst was behind us.

I have spoken at length with Doctor Robinson. You may remember that his son was killed in Sicily in the summer of 1943. He says you are suffering from Battle Exhaustion, not dissimilar to the Shell Shock which affected soldiers from the Great War. He assures me that a stay in hospital is the best course of action.

I know it's not what you want, my love. I know that. But the Doctor promises me they'll care for you and soon you'll be well and home again, and we can resume our lives and put all thoughts of these difficult years behind us. I knitted you some mittens to keep you warm; he says there are gardens for walking in, acres of gardens he said, and I want to make sure you keep warm. You just keep warm and get better Harold my love and we'll get you back home in no time.

I love you, my Darling.
Always yours,
Mildred

March 14, 1946
My most beloved,

It seems a cruel twist of fate that you came home and we were together for only three weeks. There is so much I want to tell you, and have been storing up, like a squirrel with his nuts for the long winter ahead, all through the time you've been away. I had imagined us on the settee together in the evenings, or sitting at the dinner table across from one another, or perhaps walking along the river's edge, or even holding each other in our marital bed.

Notes towards Recovery

I am so very sorry that you heard so little from me while you were away fighting. I am not sure if you understood me, last week, when I told you that we were instructed not to write. We were told by the ministry - here - I have found the exact wording: "letters from home often needlessly damage soldiers' morale." I hope now you can understand why it was I didn't write to you.

But this is no longer the belief. Doctor Robinson tells me that my letters, so long as they are full of cheerful news, can only do you well. So I shall write to you every day my Darling, and perhaps this way, share with you some of the things I have been storing up to tell you for so long.

I shall start by describing to you in detail the wedding of your sister to George...

March 15, 1946
My dearest heart,

I hope you are resting, my dear Harold. I wonder if you might have time to send me a small note to let me know that you are being well cared for, as I am beginning to doubt the wisdom of our parting again so soon after our reunion. Perhaps you would have been better off staying here, at home, where you truly belong. Maybe it is only a question of time, recovering from the nightmares which haunt you so.

But I am to write of joyful things, not my petty worries. At lunch today, at your parents' house, Susan and George announced that they are expecting a baby. Their third child! Your mother pretended to be aghast, but it was clear to all that she is pleased as punch. I suspect both she and your sister are hoping for a girl this time. When she told me I congratulated her, as I am truly happy for her good fortune. On the short walk home, however, I held my hand on my own stomach and dreamed of the day when you and I can make the same announcement. I imagine our family, of you and me at either head of the table with our children between us. Would you think me foolish if I admitted that I have already some names in mind to discuss with you? Of course if it's a boy, it should be Harold...

March 16, 1946
Dear Harold, my Love,

Because there are no secrets between us, I shall admit to you that in my deepest heart I had hoped our reunion night might have resulted in a child. Alas, it is not to be this time. When you come home, and I do pray that will be soon, we shall have many more chances to start a family.

I have not told you about my job. It might surprise you that I enjoy it so much, as when you knew me before I showed no inclination towards numbers or keeping accounts...

March 17, 1946
My Dear Harold,

I am sending this in good time to arrive for your Birthday. You see, I have not forgotten. You will think it extraordinarily extravagant of me, but I feel I have so many missed Birthdays of yours to make up for. I can make a tin of beans last me three meals, and shall continue to do so in order to send you the loveliest, softest things I can find for your to wrap yourself in, until you are back home and I can wrap you in my arms. My darling, do know that you are always wrapped in my love, and you remain at the top of my thoughts for every hour of every day.

Next year we'll throw the biggest Birthday party you can imagine...

Notes towards Recovery

March 18, 1946
My Dear Heart,

I saw the first sign of spring today, and my heart filled with joy. What do you imagine it was? A crocus, bright purple, poking above the last of the snow. It felt to me like a sign from above that good things are coming our way.

Longer letter to follow this afternoon.

With all my love,
Mildred

March 19, 1946
My Darling Harold,

I do hope that your Birthday parcel arrived. A one-line note acknowledging its receipt would calm my fears that an unscrupulous hospital worker has opened it and taken it for himself.

With all my love,
Mildred

March 20, 1946
My Dear Heart,

It is with great glad tidings that I write you to you. Your brother and sister are travelling to Toronto and will come to visit you at the hospital. I only wish I could be there too, but am giving them much to take with them to remind you of home, your home, to which I am every so hopeful they may return you. I am preparing with that great hope in mind, that I may see you as soon as Sunday night. Oh my love, I miss you so.

With all my love,
Mildred

Monday
My Dearest, my most beloved Harold,

I can barely see to write through my tears.

I will ask the hospital staff to place this, my final letter to you, in your hands in your coffin.

I am blessed indeed with the kindest sister-in-law. It can not have been easy for her, telling me the news she had to impart, but she wanted to save me for receiving a telegram from the hospital so came directly here last night.

It seems so cruel, so unfair, that after surviving the war you have been taken from us all.

Susan and I agree that it is not necessary to tell your parents the exact nature of your death. I can not bring myself to say the word out loud, and I have not stopped crying at the thought of how many demons you must have been battling to think that taking your life was the only way forward. My only consolation is that you have had my daily letters, so you have known, even in your darkest moments, that you were, you are, truly loved.

With all my love, forever,
Your Mildred

***

January, 1954
My Dear Darlene,

I am sorry we argued, but I am sure you can understand my shock, not only at your condition, but at the extraordinary lies you've been telling Doctor Scott. I think your going to this home and spending some time away will be good for both of us. I'm sorry Aunt Celia couldn't take you in, but you know how difficult it is with her husband Overseas. Doctor Scott says this home

Notes towards Recovery

comes highly recommended to him from a source he trusts. May God love and bless you despite your transgressions.
Love, Mother

February, 1954
My Dear Darlene,
I am sorry you are still so angry that you are not able to write a letter home. Your younger sister in particular misses you very much. Please send a note, if not to your father and I, then to Marion.
Love, Mother

March, 1954
My Dear Darlene,
We are having a bitterly cold winter up here and no sign of relief. Two of the cattle froze yesterday. I am working on a Victory Garden quilt. The Reverend mentioned you in his prayers and asked us to do the same. I pray for your health every night. Your father sends his love. He has forgiven you for your lapse and wishes only that when you come home we all put this episode behind us.
Love, Mother

April, 1954
My Dear Darlene,
I am truly sorry that my lasting memory of you is that last morning when you refused to meet my eyes and continued to accuse the Reverend of unspeakable acts. I imagine you are showing. I do hope you are being given milk and are looking after yourself. I understand there are good teachers there and I hope you are keeping up with your homework so when you come home you will not be behind.

I do love you, daughter.
Love, Mother

April, 1954
Dear Darlene,
Mother wouldn't give me your address. She seems to think you have to write to me first, but I copied it from an envelope when she wasn't watching. I miss you. I love you so much. When are you coming home?
Love xoxoxoxo Marion

May, 1954
Dear Darlene
Mrs. Cunningham has died. A blessing, really, she was not at all well for the past three months and suffering greatly. I made salmon sandwiches for the funeral tea but used only one tin of fish and much mayonnaise to bulk it out. I spent the housekeeping money your father gave me on two tins, however, and am enclosing the other as I know it is a favourite food of yours. I miss you my dear, and hope you will forgive my anger of those last weeks you were here.
I hope you are well and not suffering too much from ills and pains.
Love, Mother

June, 1954
Dear Darlene,
I am sure you are as glad as I am that winter is over and spring has finally arrived. Has a new home for your baby been arranged? If it is too painful for you to speak of this, I shall never mention it again.
Love, Mother

Notes towards Recovery

July, 1954
My Dear Darlene,
I am calculating that you'll be delivered of your baby this week or next and I hope you will arrive home soon after. I am enclosing a new dress for you as I'm sure you need a summer weight outfit.
Love, Mother

July, 1954
Dearest Darlene,

Please don't scold me for being a sneak, but Mother and Father started arguing the other night (something to do with the Reverend and how much tithe they pay the church) and went to their room (do they think I can't hear them?) and Mother had left her letter to you on the kitchen table. Well, it was in the envelope, but unsealed, so I opened it and read it.

A baby!

I didn't know you could have a baby before you got married, but Tessa has set me straight and now I feel like such a dolt. I don't know how you can give up your baby. Maybe you won't, but I bet you won't come home either. Tessa says you can write to me care of her address - see below - and then Mother and Father won't know that we're corresponding. Please write to me. I miss you so.
Love, Marion xoxoxox
p. s. I don't care that the Reverend has excommunicated you. He asked me to help him check for sores on his body (signs of God's displeasure at his congregation's actions, he said) after church last week and the bits of his body I had to check, all covered with white puss, smelled vile.

August, 1954
Dear Darlene,
I had the Doctor contact the home as I am no longer allowed to, your having turned eighteen. He has given me the news of the stillbirth. I hope you believe me when I tell you how truly sorry I am. Many people might think it is all for the best. I understand that it has affected your mind, and that you are staying on at the home to recover your stability. Know that I love you and wish for you only happiness and peace in your life. I do hope you will find it in your heart to forgive me and send me a note acknowledging some feelings you have for me. As a token of my love for you, I am sending you your grandmother's locket which you always loved so much.
Love, Mother

September, 1954
Dearest Darlene,
Every day I ask Tess if she has heard from you and every day she has to tell me no. The Reverend has asked me to be his Special Helper for the next Tent Revival Meeting. I suppose I have to say yes, even though I don't want to. I can't talk to Mother about this - I need my big sister here. Please write to me.
Love, Marion xoxoxoxox

October, 1954
Dear Darlene,
Every time I read about the influenza outbreak in Toronto I think of you and worry. Doctor Scott has left the town and I am at a loss of how to contact you other than at this address. I do hope you will reconsider and come home.
Love, your Mother

Notes towards Recovery

October, 1954
Darlene, my Child of Christ,
You must understand that I cannot forgive you for having broken our pact of silence because God Himself cannot forgive you. But I am concerned that you have forsaken your family. I do implore you to contact your mother, though I have told her that I fear you may have turned to sin in Toronto.
With continued prayers,
Reverend Thomas

November, 1954
Dearest Darlene,
The Reverend told me God will smite you down if I tell anyone of the sins I have performed with him. I do not understand why he speaks of my sins as he was the one who held me down behind the tent and did those things. He says I dressed provocatively and made him do things for which he is ashamed, but the next day when I wore my most modest dress, he did the same. Do not worry, I will tell no one.
Love, Marion xoxoxoxox

December, 1954
Dear Darlene,
I do not expect you can ever forgive me or your father. We now know that what you said was true. Your sister Marion has faced the same horrors at the hands of that evil man. I pray she will recover.
I beg of you to forgive us both. We know you spoke the truth. We have left the church.
With humble apologies,
and much love,
your Mother

January, 1955
Dearest Darlene,
You can come home now. It is safe. That man has left.
He made a mistake when he tried to threaten Tessa. She told her father, and had proof of what he had done to her.
I have asked her father to find you, and he has promised to do all he can. It is difficult, he says, because it was that horrible man who recommended to Doctor Scott the home you be sent to, and Doctor Scott is no longer living here. But I beg you, if you are reading this letter and have any feelings left for your family, come home.
Love, Marion xoxoxoxox

March 15, 1975
To Whom This May Concern
In the month of January 1954, my sister, Darlene Roberts, was sent to a home for unwed mothers in southern Ontario. I have no more details than that. I wonder, please, if you could check your records and see if she spent any time at City Psychiatric? I am aware that this is not - and never was - a home for unwed mothers, but as you are no doubt aware there was some confusion at that time in our history. It is a matter of urgency that I trace her movements in an effort to find her, as our mother is dying and her last wish is to see Darlene. Any help you could give me in this matter would be very much appreciated.
Yours sincerely,
Marion Roberts

***

Notes towards Recovery

To: ▉▉▉▉▉▉▉▉▉▉▉▉▉▉▉▉▉
From: ▉▉▉▉▉▉▉▉▉▉▉▉▉▉▉▉▉
Subject: City Psychiatric Basement
Sent: 5/05/09 15:53
Level: HIGHLY CONFIDENTIAL

If this is made public there will be demand for financial reparation made to victims' families. Rough estimate: 72 lockers containing letters. 394 individual pieces of luggage containing personal items. 6,829 boxes containing letters, parcels.

To: ▉▉▉▉▉▉▉▉▉▉▉▉▉▉▉▉▉
From: ▉▉▉▉▉▉▉▉▉▉▉▉▉▉▉▉▉
Subject: City Psychiatric Basement
Sent: 5/05/09 15:54
Level: HIGHLY CONFIDENTIAL

Parcels?

To: ▉▉▉▉▉▉▉▉▉▉▉▉▉▉▉▉▉
From: ▉▉▉▉▉▉▉▉▉▉▉▉▉▉▉▉▉
Subject: City Psychiatric Basement
Sent: 5/05/09 15:57
Level: HIGHLY CONFIDENTIAL

Parcels. Care packages. Knitted gloves, Bibles, tinned foodstuffs, photographs, toiletry items, gift-wrapped boxes. We haven't started an inventory as we're awaiting further directions. Clearly there is historical value to many of the documents and possibly financial worth to such things as postage stamps. But it has been suggested that disposing of it all will be the more prudent course of action.

Secrets of City Psychiatric

By H. S. Edwards
Opinion
May 6 2009

Few people would miss the irony that old 'Toronto Insane Asylum' (later the 'Hospital for Psychiatric Maladies and Nervous Disorders') was slated for demolition during this city's Mental Health Week celebrations. And while there is much to celebrate about present-day treatment for people suffering from mental health issues, we have a long way to go. In a leaked memo from one of our city councillors, it was clear that there was an unfortunate mess that needed to be disposed of. A haunted basement. Haunted, not by ghosts of those people mistreated by the psychiatric system in the past, but by the ghosts of equally mistreated families of those victims.

In the basement, bricked-over decades ago, the demolition team found lockers, luggage, and boxes of letters and parcels addressed to patients. They had never been opened, never been delivered, never been read, or worn, or enjoyed.

It makes me angry. It should make us all angry. I have read only forty-one of them, but each one broke my heart. Families, spouses, children were denied all contact with the 'inmates' as they were known until the late 1950s. These letters and parcels were their only means of contact, and that contact was never made. They contained news of weddings, births, deaths. Hope.

Notes towards Recovery

Love. Gifts. Stamps with writing paper, and angst-filled pleas for a reply. And what did our elected city councillor want to do when this discovery was made? Trace the owners or their descendants and return the items along with an apology? No. He voted to burn the evidence and pretend this had never happened, that this discovery had never been made, demonstrating, implicitly, that these people and their families never mattered a damn. (continues, page 2)

Whale Song

Spring came late to this part of northeastern Ontario. Bea stood at the winter parking spot, the top end of the lane that led down the hill to her childhood home, and looked through the jack, red and white pine forest to the lake, still frozen save for a small patch of black about two miles out, and closer, to the house, with its welcoming lights and the smell of woodsmoke. She couldn't see, but imagined the scene: her father at the kitchen table, the papers in front of him covered with mathematical equations worked out in his black pen, and her mother at the stove. The afternoon air, cold enough to freeze the hairs in her nose as she breathed in, was heavy with spruce sap, but not yet any scent of an awakening undergrowth. Still, she knelt and searched the snow, dirty with pine needles, for any hint of the first of the trailing arbutus. But it was still several feet deep and there wasn't even the tiniest sign of green poking up from the forest floor. She stood, slung her backpack over her shoulder and started down the lane. She took a deep breath. Home.

When she slid open the thick glass door her father looked up, smiled and got to his feet, and her mother reached for the cord of the stainless steel kettle. The same kettle that has always lived just there, to cover a stain on the laminate countertop; a wedding gift, repaired several times over, but never replaced. As a teenager Bea had dreamed of a house full of modern, bright, new things - now she kicked off her boots on to the knurled coir mat and ran her hand over the table where she'd eaten and drawn and done her homework and played Scrabble for the first eighteen years of her life. "Mum. Dad." She noticed the time it took for her mother to walk the short distance across the kitchen, her hand on her hip, and she noticed too her father's stooped back.

"Darling, this is a treat for us. I didn't think we'd see you again until Easter. I've put the kettle on." Her mother hugged her and her father patted her shoulder and asked her about the drive up from Toronto. How long had it taken her, were any trilliums were in bloom down south, had she seen anything interesting? No mention of the email in which Bea mentioned hour-long sessions in a therapist's sage green office and hinted at the mandated leave of absence. Instead a cup of tea and a slice of fruitcake which Bea ate as she always had, uncurling the layers of pale marzipan and icing to save for last. A roundup of the local news, a report of the last few weeks' weather and a mention of her father's upcoming talk to a group of geohydrologists in Montreal. He no longer made the four-hour round trip to Sudbury to lecture university undergrads, but continued to supervise post-graduates and speak at conferences, in places he wanted to visit, on topics he found interesting.

"So you'll give your speech in French then?" Bea teased. Her father's grade eleven report card - a bold F next to French - was a standing joke. Despite living in a Franco-Ontarian community and teaching at a bilingual university, he'd never mastered more than the very basics of his country's other language. "Darcy's Law," she said. "Q equals minus k over viscosity. What's 'viscosity' in French, I wonder?"

Her father chuckled. "It's a variation on a talk I've given before, about Leda landslides." One of her father's areas of expertise, the salt water clay - remnants of the ten thousand year old inland sea - with such unstable molecular structure that it led to silent, instant, deadly landslides. The previous spring a house just north of Montreal had disappeared into a crater in moments; the family of four were found still sitting on the sofa in front of their television.

"You'll want to stretch a bit after that long drive," said her mother. "Why don't you and Dad go for a walk before the light goes." It wasn't a question; her mother believed in the curative power of fresh air and exercise. So while her father tidied up his work Bea found a pair of fur-lined boots and hung her fashionable city coat on a hook where it would stay until the day she drove back, pulling on in its stead a pair of ski pants and a down-filled parka, knitted hat with ear flaps and thick gloves.

They set off along the shore. Tradition. The first walk when she came back was always this one - along the lakefront to Sampson's cottage on the rocky point, then up the hill and back home along the top of the escarpment.

"Mum's hip looks sore," said Bea when they were on the beach, crunching over ice-crusted drifts.

"We're getting old," her father said. "Always something falling apart." He poked his walking pole at a jagged edge of black ice and the ice shattered. "Such a mild winter. I don't think we've had more than twenty days of worthwhile skiing." He looked up into the sky and Bea knew he was considering the possibility of snowfall that night. And knew too that whatever he predicted, he'd be correct. He only had to look at the clouds, gauge the wind patterns, or smell the air and he'd know how to dress, what ski wax to use

Notes towards Recovery

Her mother had referred to the lack of cross-country skiing in an email to Bea, but not with regret. She'd reached an age, she said, when she enjoyed pottering about on skis far more than the long-distance routes their father was still fit and agile enough to tackle.

It might have been a mild winter, but Bea hunched her shoulders against the wind blowing across the lake, and was glad of the layers of heavy clothing. Everyone in Toronto complained of wind from Lake Ontario whipping up Yonge Street, but that was nothing compared to this bitterness. And out here there was no respite, no sudden rush of warm air as someone opened the door of a coffee shop, no upward whoosh of heat from a subway tunnel. But the crystal glints of the untouched snow against the washed out winter-blue sky helped compensate for the cold and Bea took a deep breath, imagining her lungs filling with the clean, northern air.

Her father stopped, pointing at the skeleton of an ash and passing her binoculars from his pocket. It took her a moment to bring the right tree into focus and search along it until she found what he'd seen: a Black-backed Woodpecker, its black and white body almost camouflaged against the winter landscape save for the yellow dot on his head. As she watched, it stripped a piece of bark, and pecked at the tawny exposed trunk. "What do you think he's looking for?" she asked.

"Some sort of beetle. Let's hope it's not an emerald ash borer."

"Is the Hairy Woodpecker still nesting in the yard?" That was the one that was easy to spot because it was so often motionless, feeling for the movement of insects under the bark. Bea kept the glasses to her eyes, watching the woodpecker continue to tap away at the tree. Baby steps, her therapist was fond of saying. Baby steps.

When they reached Sampson's cottage they cleared a patch of snow from the sloping deck and sat. From here, her parents' house was hidden, so she turned to look in the opposite direction and saw movement in the next bay over; a red truck was pulling an ice fishing hut to the shore and from the snatches of voices which were carried back, the operation wasn't going smoothly. She scanned the rest of the lake that she could see, pausing at the expanse of dark water. The hole was bigger than she'd originally judged, large enough for whitecaps to sweep across the angry surface, and she averted her gaze, focusing instead on the patterns of wind-blown snow at the lake's edge. When she was too cold not to move on she stood, and they turned inland and made their way up the hill, wading through the deep snow and weaving between spruce trees and cedars. It was hard going and they were both quiet until they reached the top, with its reward of a view all the way down the lake to the cluster of islands locals called the Binessiwi Mekuna. There were more than sixty islands, some only a few feet across, others as large as two acres and from here they did look like a negative image of the Milky Way, the dark islands dotting across the ghostly white lake.

Bea saw a flash of light from one of the smaller islands, and raised the binoculars to her eyes. All was still, save for a plume of smoke rising from the chimney of a grey weathered cottage.

"How many year-round residents left, Dad?" she asked.

"Only three this year," he said. Their names meant nothing to her. She looked one last time before they started for home, wondering at the people who didn't mind being trapped for weeks every fall when the lake was not yet frozen enough for skis or snow machine and again in the spring when it wasn't thawed enough for a canoe.

"Your mother worries about you."

Notes towards Recovery

Bea knew. Forty-three years old with a history of failed relationships and menial jobs, facing another stretch of unemployment and little hope, now, of the child-filled happily-ever-after she'd been raised to believe was everyone's right. I worry too; but she said nothing, just looked up at the trees above her.

They saw the owl at the same time. Perched on the branch of a jack pine, its beady yellow eyes stared from the mask-like face, which, ringed with black, looked like it had been stuck onto the round head as an afterthought. Bea slowly lifted the binoculars to her face and watched the owl watching her, its intense stare never wavering. She passed the glasses to her father without taking her gaze from the bird and they stood until it slowly spread its wings and flew, circling once, twice around the tips of the trees before soaring off.

"A Great Grey," her father whispered. "Well."

At home he reached down the field guide from its shelf in the kitchen and read aloud the description. Rare to uncommon in this area. "Rare to uncommon," her mother echoed as Bea opened the family log of interesting sightings. During her childhood she and her cousins had competed to see who could write the most entries; two years ago she'd re-read them all, laughing at their earnest language and enthusiastic attention to detail. Her parents' more sporadic notes still appeared - the most recent entry reported a pair of peregrine falcons. Her father had written it but her mother had added three words at the end: Peregrine - means wanderer.

"I didn't know that," said Bea. "That Peregrine means wanderer."

"So does Deirdre," said her mother.

A sharp stab of shame. "It was a canoe trip . . it went wrong," she said. "We tipped and I got caught in an eddy." She'd almost given up. "I was so worried that you'd lose another daughter to drowning." But even then she hadn't had a moment's empathy for Deirdre, and that made her feel guiltier than all the rest of it. Now she needed to not cry, so asked how she could help with dinner.

Her father lit a fire in the living room for their pre-dinner sherry. Supper was roast chicken with stuffing and gravy and creamy mashed potatoes, sweet buttered squash and broccoli with cheese sauce, followed by blueberry pie from the freezer, served with vanilla ice cream. Bea thought only briefly of the holiday pounds she'd struggled to lose, her freezer full of low-calorie meals and the hours she spent in Zumba classes, for what, she didn't know.

After supper they all read the newspaper in front of the fire. Bea knew she might be anxious to return to Toronto in two weeks, but for now, this was easy. So peaceful, to curl up on the sofa and catch up on the details she missed from her usual scan of the paper. When her mind strayed from the newsprint on the page she just stared at the multi-coloured flames as they slowly consumed the birch logs, watched the fire until it was only a hint of glowing.

In the bathroom she washed her face clean of makeup, completing the last of her transformation. She started to draw the curtains in her childhood bedroom, then paused, pressing her face against the glass to search for any sign of light from the islands. Nothing but the wind through the trees and the groaning of the ice, so she took a step back, noticing her reflection, split into two across the join of the window panes. For moment her head looked as mis-matched as the Great Grey's, not quite the right face for her body. And then she saw her eight year old self in the reflection. She raised her hands to her cheeks, feeling the skull beneath her skin and wondered how often her mother looked at her and saw flashes of Deirdre. She drew the curtains then,

Notes towards Recovery

hiding the window, muffling the lake noise so the stretching and stressing of the ice became a song of distant whales.

Her thudding heart wakes her. In a pool of sweat, she tries to call out for help but can't speak. Her throat is closing in on itself and her hand shaking too much to turn on the lamp on her bedside table. Struggling for breath, gasping at the sudden sharp pain across her chest. Heart attack. She is going to die. She stops fighting. Not so bad a death: in her childhood bed, her will is up to date, her last day has been spent with her parents and her last bite of food a summer-rich blueberry pie.

Her throat relaxed, she slowly stopped hyperventilating. She turned on the light and sat up. It wasn't her heart, it was a panic attack. She ought to have recognized it as soon as she woken in so much fear. It was always the same, when she remembered that her will was in order and she'd told her parents she loved them, the terror of dying lessened just enough to relax her and then all the other symptoms subsided. The doctor had promised her it was normal, she wasn't losing her mind. Bea didn't know.

She listened to the ice, still singing, and what might have been a wolf howl, and thought about the woodpecker, methodically searching for food, and the people alone out on their islands and the villages in Quebec and Ontario that disappeared twenty years apart, destroyed by Leda clay.

She left the bedside lamp on, and picked up a book. Baby steps. Baby steps.

It was mid-morning when she went downstairs. Her mother looked at her with concern. "You didn't sleep well, Darling."

Her parents would never push and she hadn't decided how much, if any, she'd share but when she opened her mouth she heard herself say, "It was stupid of me, just stupid. I don't know what I was thinking. I wasn't thinking." Her mother passed her a cup of coffee and dished out a bowl of porridge, adding brown sugar and cream.

"There's a child whose father is allowed to visit twice a week, supervised access only. They have to stay in the playroom, chaperoned by an access worker. He went through an acrimonious divorce and his ex-wife claimed he'd abused their son. Later she recanted her allegations and admitted she'd lied but by then it was too late, the paperwork had been filled in and the process begun. Now it will take months, longer, to undo the damage."

"It had nothing to do with me, but every time he walked past the front desk on the way out he was crying. It broke my heart."

"And so-" She paused. "I found him on an online dating site."

"I just thought if I could give them one good day out together maybe it would make it less bad." Less artificial. Bearable. And so she'd convinced him to let his ex arrange for a day pass, and she'd met the two of them, father and son, on a Tuesday with her canoe on the roof of her car and driven them to the Nith river. And it had been a good day, a great day: a gentle paddle and a picnic lunch. She'd started to believe in a real future for the three of them. But they'd gone one bend too far around the river and met an unexpected set of rapids, swollen by the spring run-off, capsizing the canoe. The boy and his father had made it out, but Bea had been caught in an eddy, pushed deeper and deeper. It was only luck that she was caught against a rock and propelled to the surface, then swept in to shore.

A quiet drive home and a terse goodbye. He wouldn't date anyone who would so recklessly put his son's life at risk. (It also transpired that he hadn't recognized her photograph on the dating site - had not connected her to the Children's Aid office. So there was that lie too.)

Notes towards Recovery

She had recovered from the hypothermia but not the nightmares. "Half-nightmare half-flashback, but all mixed up. I'm swallowing warm salt water, which makes no sense at all, and there's something pink, as well as the green canoe." Her biggest fear wasn't losing her job. "I've never been scared of water, you know that. Now I'm terrified." Even the swimming pool at her gym looked dangerous, menacing.

"It's because he's an only child. I know how lonely that can be."

"You weren't always an only child," her mother reminded her.

Bea sipped the coffee. "Children's Aid has to fire me. I broke all the rules." And she was only the receptionist, no social work qualifications, no skills beyond answering the telephone, using the photocopier. She was lucky, they said, the man in question wasn't suing her for stalking.

Silence, while her parents perhaps had to readjust ideas they held of their daughter.

"You were thinking," said her father, "that you'd try to brighten someone's life."

Her mother agreed. "Generous. Well-meaning."

"But poorly executed." Bea sighed, tried to smile. "What are your plans for today?"

Her mother said she'd like to look for the owl and wondered if Bea would take her back to the place where she and her father had seen it the previous day. They took a shortcut, a thermos of coffee, and two deck chair cushions and found the truck of a fallen tree to sit on.

Her mother asked if the therapy was helping.

"She suggests that it's self-sabotage. That I make sure I find a way to lose a job, ruin a relationship." These were things she excelled at.

"Have you told her about the other time you were scared of water?"

Bea looked at her mother. "But I've always loved swimming. I could swim before I could walk - you always told me that."

Her mother nodded. "And it's true. It's true. But the summer you were four you played on the beach all summer, you never once went into the lake."

"The summer I was four. After we came home from Italy."

"I wonder if these nightmares are about Trieste."

Bea had been three and a half when her father accepted a professorship in Italy and she recalled very little. A tiny car. A house with a courtyard. "Deirdre and I had matching swimsuits," she said, finally. "Blue and white stripes with red straps. You took us down to the seaside every day." Until.

She knew the swimsuits were a real memory because her father had taken the only photographs. In Rome, in Florence, in piazzas, with backdrops of terracotta roofs and olive trees and a pale rock wall. The sisters wore cotton dresses and posed with their arms around each other. There wasn't a single photograph of those swimsuits.

"You had a bright pink lilo," said her mother. "You both loved it." Something pink. Bea tried to conjure an image of a blow-up beach toy but couldn't. She thought perhaps Deirdre, almost six, had tried to teach her how to swim, but maybe that was a single moment misinterpreted. She knew, she was sure, her big sister had played Teacher with her as compensation for abandoning her every afternoon when she started at the local school.

And then one sunny afternoon Deirdre's class had gone on an outing to the beach and the teacher had turned her back for one minute, just one minute, and Deirdre, either misunderstanding or ignoring the instructions not to go into the sea by herself, had drowned. An accident. A moment either way and it would never have happened.

The family of three had returned to the safety of their small Northern Ontario town and Bea's few memories of her older sister had grown more and more faint.

"I didn't do enough," said her mother. "There weren't any child psychiatrists in those days. Maybe in Toronto, but not here. I thought I could just love you well again."

Bea had shocked herself at the interview for the position with Children's Aid by saying her family had never recovered from the trauma of her sister's death and she wanted to help other families do better. She'd felt a surge of guilt as she spoke, as if she had played a role in her sister's disappearance.

"You did, Mum," Bea said, reaching her mittened hand for her mother's. That was why she'd come home now. For her mother to love her well again. She looked away from the raw grief on her mother's face and then gripped her hand tighter and pointed up.

But the Great Grey owl had been watching them and was startled by Bea's sudden movement. It extended its wings and flew off, leaving only a soft shower of snow to fall from the branch and a shiver of pine needles in its wake.

ACKNOWLEDGEMENTS

Thank you Laura Stradiotto and Heather Campbell of Latitude 46 Publishing, Colette Paul, and Peter Finney. Without you this beautiful book would not exist outside my imagination.

I appreciate the financial assistance provided by the Ontario Arts Council's Writers' Work in Progress - Northern Competition. That grant was life-changing for this collection. I wrote many of these stories in Devon; thank you Charlie Hayes of Urban Writers' Retreats. Thank you Tracey Armstrong for your thoughtful and detailed feedback.

Versions of these stories appeared in the following publications: "Scraping" in *The Masters Review, Volume II*, "Notes Towards Recovery" in *Harts & Minds 1. 3*, "Push" in *Words & Women Two*, "Erratics" in *The Cardiff Review*, "Northern Lights" in *Open Minds Quarterly*, and "Fiddleback Symphony" in *Crisp*.

Thank you to my exceptional English teachers: Barbara Blanche, Bob Palmai, Skip Shand, and Denis Stokes. I am grateful to all of those with whom I have had the pleasure of discussing short stories including Gillian Beer, Ailsa Cox, Charles E. May, Daniel Menaker, Robert McGill, Valerie Purton, and Bob Thacker.

Resounding thanks to my workshop peers: Robin Kearney, Shreeta Shah, and Euan Stuart in Bath; the Angles, especially Leigh Chambers, Melissa Fu, Mary Nathan, and Kate Swindlehurst, in Cambridge; Catherine Murton Stoehr and John Picard in North Bay.

I am extremely grateful for the Breakfast Club's support as I navigate an unexpected chapter in my life: Fay and John Fowler, Marg and Jim Gleason, Donna and Dennis Landry, Diana and Paul Roy.

I am blessed to have intelligent and insightful women guiding me and sustaining me. I love you, my friends: Tiffani Angus, Penny Beck, Cindy Brownlee, Amy Crawford, Lucy Durneen, Heather Ford, Caron Freeborn, Rhoda Greaves, Kelly Saunders, Gemma Victor, and Margaret Watson. I do not have words enough to thank you, Laura Kollenberg, Maureen Patterson, and Karen Dunn Skinner, for fifty years of friendship and unfaltering faith.

Love to my family: Timothy, John, Sarah, and Jody Selander, and Tom Holden. Mum and Caroline, I owe you my deepest gratitude for your unconditional love and unwavering belief in my writing. Doug, you urged me to follow my bliss. Your steadfast confidence in me has made everything possible. (Reader, I married him. I grabbed him up, for dear life.)